W9-CFQ-172

DELILAH S. DAWSON

MINE

DELACORTE PRESS

Text copyright © 2021 by D. S. Dawson
Jacket art copyright © 2021 by Corey Brickley

Visit us on the Web! rhcbooks.com

Educators and librarians, for a variety of teaching tools, visit us at RHTeachersLibrarians.com

Library of Congress Cataloging-in-Publication Data
Names: Dawson, Delilah S., author.
Title: Mine / Delilah S. Dawson.
Description: First edition. | New York : Delacorte Press, [2021] | Audience: Ages 8–12. | Summary: "Twelve-year-old Lily moves to a creepy old house in a Florida swamp and finds out that the house isn't empty: it's packed full of the previous occupants' trash, keepsakes, and, Lily begins to suspect, maybe even their ghosts"— Provided by publisher.
Identifiers: LCCN 2020031262 (print) | LCCN 2020031263 (ebook) | ISBN 978-0-593-37322-4 (hardcover) | ISBN 978-0-593-37323-1 (library binding) | ISBN 978-0-593-37324-8 (ebook)
Subjects: CYAC: Moving, Household—Fiction. | Ghosts—Fiction. | Family life—Florida—Fiction. | Souvenirs (Keepsakes)—Fiction. | Florida—Fiction.
Classification: LCC PZ7.D323 Min 2021 (print) | LCC PZ7.D323 (ebook) | DDC [Fic]—dc23

The text of this book is set in 11.25-point Apollo MT Pro.
Interior design by Cathy Bobak

Printed in the United States of America
10 9 8 7 6 5 4 3 2 1
First Edition

This book is for Florida.
Florida knows why.

1.

LILY HORNE WAS DYING.

Literally dying.

Okay, maybe not literally.

But very, very theatrically.

"This is the end!" she gasped, swooning as much as her seat belt would allow. "World . . . going dark. Can't breathe . . ."

She took a moment to try out various moaning and gagging sounds, making sure she had the absolute attention of her audience, before naturally pivoting into the dramatic death that always made her cry.

"I was aiming for the sky," she sang, low and questioning, following it up with a sputter.

"Oh God, no more *Hamilton*," her mom moaned.

With a final gasp, Lily went rigid, eyes flown wide in shock and terror, then exhaled and let her bones melt so that her body

went limp and unnaturally twisted, held up only by the con-
stricting seat belt. Waiting for a reaction, she kept her breaths
completely silent, her chest barely moving—a trick she'd
learned from a video by a corpse actor on YouTube—a guy
who actually got paid to pretend to be dead. A little morbid,
maybe, but it helped her land the part of Juliet last summer—
and gave her a new possible career goal.

"You're fine," her dad said, pretending to be cheerful despite the fact that he was talking with his teeth clenched together. He glanced at her mom, who was quietly crocheting in
the passenger seat, her head studiously down as she tried to
avoid having this argument. Again. "Right, Laura?"

Mom looked up. "It's going to be great," she recited wood-
enly. "A new beginning."

When Dad sighed, it was understood that he was disappointed in everyone—in Lily for being Lily, and in her mom
for putting her in that first preschool production of *Peter Pan*
and awakening her overly dramatic nature.

Would they respond this way, Lily wondered, if she were
actually dying? Having a panic attack? Or a heart attack? If she
just curled up and expired in the backseat without any of her
telltale theatrics?

If so, they'd be sorry they hadn't paid more attention.

As it was, she'd been sighing and flouncing and swooning and groaning around the house in obvious misery for
weeks, ever since Dad had announced that they'd be moving

to Florida. Lily didn't want to move to Florida because it was an awful place and her new school probably wouldn't have a drama club, or even a stage. Her internet searches had revealed that there wasn't a local theater in their new town.

She'd loved everything about Boulder, Colorado, from the audaciously wide skies and tall mountains to the startlingly sudden snowstorms and the fields full of popcorning prairie dogs. She'd especially loved their local playhouse—which was an actual Quonset hut, according to the many informational placards she'd read in the hallways over the years while in line to audition. She'd never wanted to leave—until she departed for New York or Hollywood. Now the deeper south they drove, leaving her entire world behind, the worse she felt. Colorado was full of bright surprises, but Florida seemed so old and withered. Everything here was too hot and shriveled to do anything but make swampy fart sounds.

Lily wouldn't even let herself think about the reason they'd had to leave. Her dad kept insisting Florida was a chance to start over, so when she saw the blue Florida sign with the oranges on it, she closed her eyes and lifted her feet to jump into her new life. She felt it, the exact moment they crossed that invisible border. It was as if a barrier resisted her slightly, as if the hot summer sun rejected exactly who she was, or at least wanted to punish her for rejecting it first. When she put her feet down, she felt no victory.

The miles rolled by and the car inched along the cracked,

lonely highway, deeper and deeper into central Florida, an adventurer crawling toward death in a desert while vultures circled overhead. Unlike the rush of stage jitters, this panic sat in her belly, heavy as a lump of cafeteria pizza that should've been good but was actually terrible.

"Just a few more miles," Dad said, even though it was perfectly obvious, thanks to the map app on his phone in its stand on the dashboard.

The setting sun slashed viciously through the car windows, and Lily tried to shrink away, as her pale skin sunburned easily. But with the rest of the backseat packed so tightly with bags and boxes, there was nowhere to hide. She was stuck. All the things she wanted—comfort, choice, freedom, the ability to be her overly dramatic self—had been taken away.

The motion sickness medicine they'd given her every four hours had worn off, and her cell phone was almost out of battery. She couldn't even text her best friend, CJ, back in Colorado. The only thing she wanted more than for the car to stop was for Dad to just turn the old sedan around and head straight back to their empty house, the house where she'd grown up, where she knew and loved every brick, and where she'd arranged her big walk-in closet into a stage. But she knew better than to say that out loud. Every time she brought up Colorado, her dad's face went red, and his mouth pinched down, and he looked away. She couldn't remember the last time he'd genuinely smiled at her.

"Are you excited back there?" he asked with the forced cheerfulness of a mall Santa. He'd been that way ever since he'd accepted the new job in Tampa, as if saying that this was a good move for the family a hundred times a day could make it true. His acting skills were extremely subpar.

"No. I told you: I'm dying," Lily answered. "My heart—"

"You're not dying. You've got to stop being so melodramatic. We talked about this."

But . . . Lily's entire life revolved around being dramatic, and . . . well, the panic wasn't too far from the truth. She was out of Colorado for the first time ever, destined to die of an exploded heart in the state that—to her—only existed because of Disney World. She didn't know anyone here, her parents were always angry at each other, her dad was always annoyed with her, and she had an entire summer to sit around, worrying about what would happen when she started eighth grade at a school that probably had no drama club and no fall musical.

And although she'd asked to see pictures of the new house, her parents had only shown her one—of the outside. Which meant there was something wrong with it. Her room was probably super tiny and didn't have a closet.

Finally they turned off the highway, cruising past palm trees and plants that looked like giant pineapples.

"This is Land O' Lakes," her mom said—the first thing she'd spontaneously offered in hours. She couldn't even pretend to sound excited. "Our new home."

They passed stores and chain restaurants and, surprisingly, cows. The sun began to set, fiery orange and pink against a sky gone the soft purple of milk left in a bowl after eating marshmallow cereal. The streetlights came on as the car entered a residential area, and Lily noticed that most of the homes here hid behind high wrought-iron fences and heavy stone walls, like medieval citadels constantly under fire. Beyond the black bars, she sometimes caught a glimpse of kids riding bikes or swimming in pools surrounded by weird cages made out of screens.

But her dad didn't turn the car into any of these comfortable, walled-off communities. He put on his blinker and slowed to turn down a mangy dirt road flanked by sharp bushes nestled in sand. Scrubby forest hid what lay beyond, and the headlights flashed over low branches dripping with grotesque gray moss that looked like witch hair.

"Don't touch that stuff," her mom said. "It's full of lice."

"Mites," Lily corrected. She'd Googled all the ways to die in Florida so that she'd be prepared.

Mom's voice quavered like she was going to cry. "Just don't touch it."

Up ahead, a shape appeared amid the trees, and Lily recognized the building she'd seen in that one picture on Dad's phone. The house was brown and angular and strange, with sloping roofs and big windows—it almost looked like it was half buried underground. Just in front of it, a bright blue dumpster sat, the only hard, colorful object in a sea of rustling shadows.

But the house didn't quite match that picture she'd seen, either. It looked . . . sadder. The gutters were stuffed with leaves and the sprouts of baby trees, the fence was falling down, weeds were growing knee-high, and an old recliner sat out front with stuffing exploding out of squirrel-chewed holes. The car rolled to a halt, and Lily realized that the house didn't look like it was all shined up for sale—it looked like it had been abandoned years ago.

"What's wrong with it?" she asked.

Her mom sighed, and her dad quietly but firmly said, "It just needs a little TLC."

"Tender loving care," her mom said, glancing at Lily's confused face. "It was a bank sale. We have to clean it out."

"Hence the dumpster," Lily finished with great gravitas. "We bought a dumpster house."

Dad ignored that and got out first, leaving the headlights on and his door open. Mom sniffled as if sucking down a sob, picked up her purse and yarn bag, and got out, too. When Lily didn't budge, her dad opened the back door for her and said tightly, "Stop this moody nonsense and get out of the car. It's not that bad. You just always have to make everything into such a big production."

Lily flinched. He always talked to her now as if she did

everything specifically to annoy him. He used to smile at her, eyes twinkling, like he didn't quite understand her but was still fond of her. But not anymore, not after the night last winter when . . .

Nope. Lily wouldn't let herself think about it.

She raised her chin, undid her seat belt, and scanned the darkness out beyond the house, where tall trees and pointy-leaved bushes crowded close, their shadows shifting restlessly beyond reach of the car's headlights. Two green sparks flashed and disappeared into the brush.

Eyes.

Lily had read that the animals in Florida were somehow wilder than elsewhere, like they hadn't changed much since the time of the dinosaurs. Burmese pythons and other big snakes bred in the wild here and terrorized the swamps, and the trees were drooping with big cats and murderous birds. She wondered what kind of strange creature lived out there, one foot on her property and the other in the wilderness.

She stepped out of the car. The heat settled on her like a wet, suffocating blanket, and a drop of sweat trickled down her face. Her long dark hair felt heavy on her neck. Thunder rumbled threateningly, shaking the ground, and the sounds of the night bore down on her, a chorus of hums and peeps and screeches unlike anything she'd ever known in Colorado. It sounded like a pet store. She couldn't see a single neighboring house from here, and yet somehow this place felt too hot, too crowded, too heavy, too loud, pressing in on all sides. When she looked at the building before her, an odd numbness crept down her arms. It just felt . . . wrong. Every instinct urged her to unleash a stage scream, the kind that would rattle down her throat and make adults finally take notice.

But she didn't, in part because she didn't want to give those green eyes any indication that she was a frightened prey animal, and in part because her dad was already mad and, like the night, just looking for a reason to boil over.

Lily had the distinct feeling the house was going to open its mouth and swallow her whole. She felt tiny and helpless, and she hated that. The fear turned to bubbling anger—at her parents for bringing her here, at herself for what she'd done to start this chain of events, and at Florida for being . . . Florida. She threw herself back into the car, slamming the door shut and crossing her arms.

"I wish I was dead," she growled.

She didn't really, not quite.

She just didn't want to be here.

2.

HER PARENTS DIDN'T EVEN TRY TO SWEET-TALK HER INTO GETTING OUT of the car. In fact, they completely ignored her protests, no matter how obviously she fumed. Without AC, the car swiftly became a sweatbox, and Lily finally got out, slung her backpack over her shoulder, and stuck her phone in the back pocket of her jean shorts.

The driveway was gravel, but the walkway to the house crunched strangely beneath her Converse—gritty like sand but sharp like shells. The air was so hot and wet that it was like standing in the bathroom after someone took a long shower. Lily noticed a lake out back, the water flat and black. The sound from that direction was an eerie chorus of humming and buzzing. She felt a strange tickle, and looked down to see a huge mosquito brazenly drinking from her hand. Fascinated, she watched it for a moment before smacking it, leaving behind a gray smear and a trickle of blood.

"Got it!" Dad crowed, holding up a ring of keys. He had been struggling to get the front door open while her mother played some farm game on her phone with nervous intensity, her usual way of avoiding conflict.

The door creaked open, and a thick, rotten smell rolled out with a puff of hot, dry air, as if the house was an old man who'd been holding his breath. When a light clicked on, Lily's jaw dropped, and she finally understood everything—why there had been no pictures, how they'd been able to afford a house at all after her dad had been out of work for so long.

It was a hoarder's house.

A hoarder's house . . . that had been abandoned.

And now it was *their* house.

"Oh my *God*," she said, holding her nose. "I'm going to puke."

Towers of newspapers and magazines and catalogs and old mail and black garbage bags wobbled just inside the door, blocking the overhead light. Dirt and hairballs and crusted brown socks dusted the wood floor. It was a big room, an open sort of den that led into a small kitchen, but it was claustrophobically cluttered with a mountain of trash.

"You promised it wouldn't be this bad," Mom muttered.

"Jack said it wouldn't be," her dad said, desperately trying to cling to his fake optimism. "The house itself is in good condition. Good bones. There's nothing wrong with it structurally. We just have to do some cleaning up."

"*We?*" Lily growled, her throat tight. "How much can *we* do before you start your jobs? You guys get to go to work all day, and I have to stay home alone all summer in this . . . this . . . stanky trash heap!" She wished there was a convenient couch she could throw herself on, but the couch was buried in garbage bags and looked as wet and soft as a mushroom, so she just fluttered her hands around in annoyance and tried to breathe through her mouth.

"We don't *get* to go to work." Her dad turned to glare at her, his shoulder knocking into a pile of boxes, causing it to tumble over and making Lily dance back. "We *have* to go to work. And this negative attitude is only going to make it harder for everyone."

Mom pulled Lily to her side and squeezed her shoulders. "I have a few weeks off and then a part-time schedule at the urgent care at first, remember? I wouldn't leave you alone with . . . this."

As Lily looked around at the deluge of garbage, she saw her summer disappear before her eyes. She was twelve, and school was out, which meant that she was free labor. And there was nothing she could do about it. And her dad's last dig at her attitude was a good reminder that if she had any hope of getting what she wanted—theater camp, some kind of pet, the chance to go back to Colorado—she had to play nice.

Luckily, she'd seen *Mary Poppins* so many times that she

could easily paste on a chipper smile and can-do attitude, even if she felt horrible on the inside.

"Where's my room?" she asked.

"You get the whole upstairs to yourself," Dad said. "Although maybe it's more of a loft than an entire floor. The realtor told me it was the cleanest part of the house. Should be some stairs around here. Just let me hit some more lights."

He fiddled with the switches, and Lily's mom said a bad word when the full horror of the house was revealed. No surface was clean or empty. There was clearly furniture somewhere under there, but it was hidden by dust and cobwebs and . . . stuff. Greasy pizza boxes were piled to the ceiling in one corner, magazines moldered in limp towers, and Amazon boxes were stacked haphazardly everywhere—hundreds, maybe thousands of them.

"We passed that hotel by the highway—" Mom started, soft and tentative.

"There's the stairs," Dad said firmly, having already shot down the idea when they passed said hotel, claiming that now every dollar counted as he glared at Lily in the rearview mirror.

Lily knew there was no hope, so she stepped around a pile of newspapers—who even read newspapers anymore?—and over a black-stained towel glued to the floor. The wooden stairs, amazingly, were empty. Not clean, of course, but not being used to store more junk. She hurried upstairs, noting that the air, at least, felt cleaner up there. At the top of the stairs, she looked down in disgust at the mounds of stuff on the first floor that she'd have to start moving tomorrow, at the piles of polo shirts and pants still on hangers and the leaning towers of bottled waters. Her parents stood amid the garbage like strangers lost in some new city with odd customs. Her mother went back to her phone, and her father just rubbed his beard and shrugged like it was someone else's problem. Which, Lily understood, it now was—hers and her mom's.

She turned away. Whatever was up here had to be better than what her parents had to deal with down there. If the master bedroom was anything like the den, it wasn't going to be fun finding a spot big enough and clean enough to let them both lie down and get some sleep without touching literal garbage.

Opening the door at the top of the stairs and flicking on the overhead light, Lily was pleasantly surprised: The room was free from hoarder junk. There was an old daybed with rumpled covers and a collection of meticulously placed stuffed animals, a stand with a small TV and a gaming system, some bookshelves, and a dresser. Much to her horror, the dresser held a glass terrarium with a screen top, and within it lay a dead snake, curled in a spiral of bones and rot.

Once her initial shock wore off, she edged closer and peered inside. She wasn't squeamish, and she thought snakes were interesting, if a bit inconvenient, as long as they weren't out in the yard and trying to kill her. The sight was strange and beautiful, in its way, the snake coiled on its back, ragged bits of scaled orange skin rippling over visible bones. The poor thing. Left here, trapped without water or food or a way out. Her eyes traced the edges of the room, considering how long the house must've sat empty. And wondering why anyone would leave it that way, as if they'd just closed the door and walked away.

She decided it had to be years. Which meant that the sheets on "her" bed were years beyond detergent, which wasn't okay. She opened the small closet and quickly closed it again when all she found were dirty clothes and old, broken toys. There was nothing upstairs but a small landing and her room, definitely no linen closet, so she had to find her parents and ask about sheets, a blanket—even a garbage bag, at this point. Anything to keep her skin from touching those pee-yellow pillows and sheets. She was halfway down the stairs and just about to yell out to her mom when she heard her parents arguing again.

"Look, this was a good deal. An investment. We're lucky Jack found it—" Dad was saying.

"And what kind of commission did your frat brother make on this garbage heap?" Mom sighed. "You promised me it wouldn't be a money pit." Her voice was ragged, exhausted.

"It's not," Dad snapped. "This is all cosmetic. The dumpster is already here. We've just got to make it work. All our savings—"

"I know. But we didn't look upstairs first. Do you think there's any sign of . . . what happened?"

The pause sat so heavily that Lily could hear the dust settle.

"It happened downstairs," Dad said firmly. "It was natural. Jack said the upstairs was fine."

Lily couldn't take it anymore.

"Mom? Do we have any sheets? This bed is super gross."

Her mom appeared at the bottom of the stairs, looking lost and a little apologetic. "Somewhere in the car . . . I just need to . . . maybe there's a closet?" She waved her hands, pantomiming that her brain was so overwhelmed that she'd forgotten how to find sheets.

Lily went downstairs. Since she knew there was nothing in the den, she passed right by her mom and into a narrow hallway. Underneath all her theatrics, Lily was a logical person, and logic suggested that the best place to find blankets would be a closet near the master bedroom, or possibly shelves in the laundry room. But of course when she found the closet, everything in it was old and smelled like mildew. As she rummaged between some threadbare towels that had once been white, something fat and dark dropped on her hand, heavy as a grape. Lily screamed and jerked her hand back. The biggest roach she'd ever seen plopped off onto a towel and skittered back into the shadows as if she'd offended it.

"What's wrong?" her mom called—without coming any closer.

"It's raining giant, gross roaches!" she shouted back. "This place is awful!"

"That's enough of that attitude!" her dad boomed with, she noted, an awful lot of attitude.

Lily wanted to get out of his line of fire and had to wash her hands, so she opened the door to what she hoped was the downstairs bathroom. She was right, and it was relatively clean, aside from a stack of old *Prevention* magazines and a scuzzy black comb. The water sputtered brown when she turned on the faucet and the old soap dispenser was cloudy with a clogged pump, but she managed to wash her hands, grateful at least that the water was hot enough to scour off the feeling of roach feet.

But when she glanced into the toilet bowl, she found something she didn't understand. It was full of wet ashes and the remains of photographs. Dozens of them, mounded together, their edges burned black and the water glistening among flashes of shoulders and hands, of what looked like a woman and child—but no faces.

The faces had all been burned away.

Lily backed away from the toilet, shivering, her breath coming in real gasps, her heart stuttering in her chest. Whatever this was, it wasn't normal.

She thought about telling her parents, but she could hear them arguing elsewhere in the house, trying to keep it quiet so they wouldn't worry her. Funny how they always said that—that they didn't want to worry her—but when she was *really* worried, they either told her she was being melodramatic or ignored her completely, like now.

The last leg of the car trip had been a long one, and now that she was here, she had to pee. At least it seemed like there were no bodily fluids already in the bowl. She held her breath and reached into the toilet with both hands, pulling out the photos and dumping them into an old metal trash can, which was half full of used tissues and other garbage. When the bowl was empty, she washed her hands again. After she'd done her business and washed her hands a third time, she stared at the garbage can, noting that water was leaking out of its rusted bottom. The photos were just too creepy; she felt an urge to get them out of the house.

Even though she was terrified of more roaches, she picked up the garbage can between two fingers, hurried to the front door without a glimpse of her parents, fiddled with the outside lights, and walked fast to the dumpster. It seemed much taller now than it had when they'd first pulled up, and she almost dumped the photos in the dirt yard to deal with tomorrow. But something about them—they needed to be out of sight.

Taking a deep breath, Lily climbed a few rungs of the ladder built into the side of the dumpster and upended the trash can, letting the wet photos splatter against the metal far below. Then, on second thought, she chucked the trash can in, too. It landed with a heavy clank, and something down there rustled like it was alive and mad. Lily jumped off the ladder and ran back to the open front door, holding her breath the entire time.

A soft whine caught her attention, and she spun to stare into the woods, right where she'd seen the green flash of eyes earlier. Something moved, and she squinted as a shadow detached itself from the forest and took a few halting steps toward her. It was taller than a raccoon or possum, more upright than a gator, and bigger than a cat. Was it . . . maybe . . . a dog?

"Here, boy," she called, and the creature paused.

"Lily, what are you doing?" her dad asked from inside.

The shape slunk back into the forest, and she went inside and closed the door.

"Just tossing some junk," she said. "That's what I'm supposed to be doing, right?"

His lips pressed together; he hated it when she walked the fine line between polite and talking back, but sometimes she couldn't stop her mouth. "Look, I've had enough with—" He closed his eyes and took a deep breath, fighting for control of his temper. "It's late. You'll have plenty of time to clean tomorrow."

She nodded and scurried upstairs without a word. When Dad got mad, it was better to just stay out of his way—he had one of those voices that only had two modes, soft and reasonable or a dominating, furious shout, and lately it had all been shouting. She'd found no blankets or towels that she was willing to touch, and she would have to get past her dad to find her mom, so she curled up on the floor with her head pillowed on her backpack, miserable and uncomfortable and willing herself not to cry.

Only later, when she woke up in absolute silence and utter darkness, did it occur to her that if the house had been closed up for years or even months, all those photos should've been a dingy gray mass of waterlogged pulp, their images long faded away.

But no—they'd been as bright and crisp as if they'd been printed that day.

Aside from the burned bits.

The burned faces.

3.

LILY WOKE UP, IN A WORD, BADLY.

On most summer mornings, she opened her eyes in her own comfortable bed back in Boulder, the sun outlining her window with molten gold. Today, she woke up on the floor, covered in sweat and dust, hot and aching and as cranky as she was when she had the flu. Between the heat and the humidity, she began to think that maybe living in Florida just felt like being sick all the time.

Lily knew her friends back in Colorado were jealous and thought moving to Florida would be amazing, like being on vacation every day. As it turned out, life in the Sunshine State was not all swimming at the beach with dolphins before eating dinner with princesses at Disney.

Her room wasn't much better by the light of morning. It looked like some other kid had simply walked out one day and never come back. The fan wobbled like crazy if she turned it up too high, and the air-conditioning didn't seem to do much—the air was still and thick, almost choking. The blinds were dusty and bent and didn't block the sun's light or heat. Before her mother could set her to work on something downstairs, she quietly poked around, trying to understand more about whoever had lived here before her.

Like the sheets, the walls were light yellow, and the comforter had once been white with pastel polka dots but was now the color of old piano keys. There were two printed canvases on the wall, one showing an elephant and the other a llama. The video game system by the TV was an older one, and there were plenty of games, but the TV wouldn't turn on.

When she opened the drawers in the dresser, she discovered that a little girl had lived here. And she was younger and smaller than Lily was, judging by the T-shirts—maybe eight years old, by Lily's guess. She'd been neat, whoever she was, with all her shirts, shorts, and jeans carefully folded. A series of uniforms were in the bottom drawer, polos in navy and white and a variety of khaki bottoms. Lily's mom had told her that most of the schools here had some kind of uniform. She wasn't looking forward to that part. Being the same as everyone else—well, the thought made her wrinkle up her nose. Even if she'd been forced to promise her dad she'd tone down her attitude, she wasn't sure if it was possible to completely change who she was—or even act like she had changed all that much. All she knew was that she'd promised she would try.

She went to the bookshelf and nosed around some more. Unfortunately, the books were mostly chapter books for younger readers, not the contemporary YA stories Lily liked. There were a few bigger fantasy novels that didn't have their covers cracked yet, plus the kind of boring classics that well-meaning elderly relatives offered up at Christmas along with stale candy and fuzzy socks. On a hunch, Lily picked up a few of the books and soon found what she was looking for written inside the front cover of a Magic Tree House book . . .

The kid's name was Britney.

Britney West.

And now Lily was seriously curious about her. Britney seemed like an organized kid—and yet she'd left all her stuff here. And let her snake die. If Lily's parents had let her have a pet, there was no way on earth she would leave it behind. But maybe it hadn't been Britney's fault. Maybe her parents had swept her away against her will, just like Lily's had—but with even less notice or choice.

"Well, Britney. Let's see if you left any secrets," Lily said softly.

Lily checked behind all the books, ran her fingertips along the inside edges of the drawers, even got on her hands and knees to check the empty space under the daybed, but all she found was dust. No diary, no computer, no jewelry box, no loose wooden floorboard that lifted up to reveal hidden trinkets. No trophies, awards, or photos. Just a couple of safety pins and the clear plastic tags that came with new clothes.

"Sorry, but you were boring," she told the room.

Heading downstairs, she steeled herself to see the house for the first time in daylight. The den would've been airy and full of light from the huge windows if not for all the looming junk and the heavy, once-white curtains that Lily knew her mother would get rid of immediately. The front door was open, and the newspaper stacks were already disappearing. Outside, Lily heard the thump of something heavy landing in the dumpster. So much for checking out the photos she'd tossed last night—judging by the path her mom had left behind in the big room, the photos were already buried.

With the photos out of reach, Lily was ready to get down to business, just so she wouldn't have to look at the garbage anymore. Better to do something than nothing. And maybe, just maybe, if she was super helpful and showed that she'd changed her attitude, there might be a chance they could go back home.

"I brought doughnuts," her mom said, appearing in the door in old sweats with her dark hair up in a bandanna. She smiled a smile that said *Everything is terrible and we both know it, but we have to pretend so we don't cry,* and in return Lily gave her a tight, pinched smile that said *Yes, and it's all your fault because you're the adult and you didn't stop it from happening, even if we both know it's really my fault.*

"Dad's already at work?" she asked, taking a chocolate glazed doughnut.

"I dropped him off. We need the car." Mom put her hands on her hips and frowned at the house, hard-core. "First, we need a grocery list." She pulled out her phone and murmured, "Garbage bags . . ."

"Gloves," Lily added.

Her mom nodded. "Gloves. Paper towels. Cleaning spray. Toilet paper."

"Sheets, blankets, and towels."

At that, Mom's jaw dropped open and she went red with guilt. "Oh no. You asked, and I completely forgot. There was just so much going on last night. Your stuff is still in the trunk. Honey, I'm so sorry. It's just the drive, and this place, and your father . . ." She trailed off and shook her head. "Anyway, yes, we have sheets for you. Is your bed . . ." She trailed off.

Lily breathed out hard through her nose. Of course they'd forgotten her.

"Gross and covered in someone else's dandruff and dead skin mites? Yes. So can we please unload the car?"

The move had been so sudden that they'd been forced to pack everything into a big portable storage container. Until it arrived in Florida, all they had was what fit into the sedan. And most of that was Dad's work clothes, as his job was the most important thing they had going on this summer and her mom just wore nurse's scrubs. Lily had a backpack full of clothes, a shopping bag full of books and yarn, and that was it. Even her bike had gone in the container. She was pretty much trapped here, and she was already clearly last on the list of things to care about, which hurt, but . . . well, it was a familiar kind of hurt, a kind of hurt she was accustomed to shoving down.

Parents capable of ignoring the big, dramatic outbursts were of course going to completely miss something as small and quiet as run-of-the-mill hurt feelings.

Lily wanted a hug, but her mom was too busy, so she just had another doughnut before they ran to the store for supplies. She was actually surprised by how nice the superstore was, clean and white and well lit, but then she remembered that Florida was a regular place where most people lived regular lives; it was just *her* house that was icky and old and dark and hidden by a swamp. She saw a couple of other kids there, all in shorts and flip-flops, but it's not like anybody made friends at the store.

It was barely lunchtime when they got back, and the temperature was already hotter than the hottest day of her life in Colorado. The air felt heavy, pressing down on every inch of her skin. Yesterday's clothes began to itch, but it's not like she'd brought anything better. Florida was no place for denim in June.

Wearing yellow rubber gloves that went over her elbows, Lily helped her mom with the newspapers and magazines until all the piles by the front door were gone. Then they focused on the kitchen, trying to clear years of dishes and garbage off the counters and get the sink and oven and microwave clean. It was gross but satisfying work, but it was also far from over.

Late in the afternoon, Lily took a few black trash bags upstairs to empty out the clothes in her dresser and closet. Her mom wanted to donate the clothes, but they looked stained and faded with time. Instead, she tossed them in a bag along with the stuffed animals, which showed a lot of wear and love. There was a big, floppy brown horse, a gray hippo, a lone teddy bear, a doll who'd received a bad haircut, and a pink bunny with long, ragged ears and red thread unraveling from some words embroidered on its belly. Lily didn't look too closely—she felt bad for these toys that had once been beloved and were now forgotten and being banished. As soon as they were all in the bag, she tied it closed and hurried out to toss it in the dumpster before she changed her mind. Instead of climbing up the ladder, she just flung the bag in, satisfied to hear it land with a soft thump.

Back upstairs, she wasn't sure about the bed—it was nicer than her old one, which sagged—so she stripped off the sheets and tossed the pillows. The mattress, at least, was clean and pretty new. But it still felt a little too personal, so she heaved the bare mattress up to flip it over to the fresh side.

MINE

The mattress flopped down with a thump and a puff of dust.

When Lily stood back to make sure this side was also free from somebody else's pee stains, she found something strange.

The word *MINE* had been angrily scrawled on the white fabric in dark gray. When she touched the letters, they smeared. As if they'd been written in charcoal.

Or ashes.

4.

"MOOOOOM!" LILY SCREECHED. WHEN HER MOTHER DIDN'T COME pounding up the stairs like anyone hearing their kid panic should, she shouted, "Ugh! Mom! For real! You have to see this!"

Less quickly than she would've preferred, her mom arrived, still wearing her long yellow gloves and looking exhausted and already over everything. She stopped on the stairs, just close enough so they wouldn't have to yell.

"What's wrong?"

"Come look at my mattress." Lily stood beside it, pointing down at that stark gray word that had no business being there.

"It's just an old mattress. Our furniture will be here soon."

"But it says—"

Too late. Her mom was already headed downstairs.

Lily groaned and leaned back against the wall. She knew

that her mom was distracted, and she also knew that if she called her back upstairs, her mood would go straight to anger, and then she'd tell Dad.

With a creeping sense that she was being watched, Lily brushed off the random word on the mattress, dusted the gray powder off her gloves, and tried to forget it had ever existed. Maybe her mom was right—it was just a gross old mattress, and it probably didn't matter.

It didn't take long before her room was in decent shape, especially after she'd chucked the entire terrarium into the dumpster. She should've done it last night, but she was so exhausted that she forgot. Now it gave her the willies. It was heavy and awkward, and she had to move it down the stairs one step at a time. She thought about burying the snake somewhere, but . . . it was just too much. She couldn't stop imagining reaching her hand into the glass box and the dead, dry snake coming alive, sinking thick yellow fangs into her arm.

She settled for singing "Pore Jud Is Daid" from *Oklahoma!* as she tipped the glass over the side of the dumpster. The glass didn't even break when it hit the mound of black bags, and Lily wished she had looked earlier, to see if the photographs were still there. So much about this place was just wrong: the photos, the roach, the snake, the word on the mattress. Her head felt crowded and thick, and her heart jittered worryingly.

She climbed down from the dumpster and jumped up and down on the ground for a few minutes, muttering "Unique New York" and "Red Leather, Yellow Leather" until everything felt normal and grounded again, just like Miss Cora had taught her the first time she had stage fright.

She knew her mom was busy emptying out the horrific fridge, and Lily very much didn't want to be called in to help with that particular job, so she walked around the house to examine the rest of the property. It had been too dark to really see last night, but by the light of day, it seemed very pretty, if wildly overgrown. There were woods off to the right and a lake straight ahead with a small, dilapidated dock. Beyond the tall wooden fence on the right hid one of those strange pool cages she'd seen on the drive, reminding her of the romantic glass conservatories in old movies about England. Which, she realized, meant they might have a pool.

Finally, something to be excited about! Lily fussed with the rusty latch on the fence gate and had to shove the warped wooden door open. The good news was that they did indeed have a pool. The bad news was that their pool was half full of dark green sludge and wet black leaves. The screens overhead were ripped and dangling like cobwebs, and the two patio chairs were rusted into contorted shapes. A string of fat-bulbed Christmas lights was strung around the edges of the cage, but when she let herself inside and plugged them in, only three of the bulbs lit up. She walked around the stained concrete and let herself out the other screen door.

On the opposite side of the pool was a garden with misshapen pineapples and orange and lemon trees, most of their fruit covered in powdery black gunk. Beyond that, the lake seemed to merge into a swampy area with lots of trees with tall roots that poked up through the water like wooden knives. Lily poked a dangling orange. Again, she felt like she was being watched, but there were no visible neighbors.

"Hello?" she called.

Of course there was no answer.

But this was her house, which meant that these were her oranges. She reached out to cup one, unsure how to know if it was ripe.

Plunk.

Lily staggered. Another orange had fallen, conking her right on the head.

"Guess that one's ripe," she muttered, picking up the fallen fruit.

But when she punctured the dimpled skin with her thumb, it was even more bad news: grapefruit.

After chucking the grapefruit far out into the water of the lake—because it was obviously biodegradable—she put a toe of her sneaker on the dock and pressed down. It was an old, rickety thing, about twice as big as a twin bed, and it creaked and splashed under her weight. A small rowboat bobbed beside it with two splintery gray oars rattling around on the bottom, along with a few inches of sludgy water.

The dock wobbled precariously underfoot, and Lily practically leapt back on land. She wasn't the strongest swimmer.

"I don't think I'm gonna like it here," she sang softly in her best *Annie* voice.

Somewhere to her right, a twig snapped, and her head jerked up.

"Who's there?"

The only answer was a soft whine, just like she'd heard last night.

She glanced back at the house to make sure her mom was still inside, since her mom believed that all animals were carriers of disease, or at least riddled with parasites. Lily was constantly begging for a pet, but her mom had always said no.

"Hey, good dog. You out there?" she said in a softer voice.

Another twig snapped, and then something crunched around in the dead leaves. She walked toward the sound, slowly, picking up a thick stick in case it was something rabid. Or a gator, which she'd heard just waddled around Florida roads and golf courses whenever they pleased.

"Come on, pupper," she encouraged. "I won't hurt you."

Something shivered in the forest, right on the edge of the shadows under the brush and trees. It was taller than knee-high and strangely shaped, awkward and shaggy, an indiscriminate shade of dirt brown.

"Come on, now," she called sweetly.

It stepped out of the shadows, just a little, trembling, and she realized that maybe under all that gunk, it actually was a dog. But not a house dog that anyone cared about—it was totally matted and tangled with vines and twigs and mud.

"Hey, good boy."

At that, the dog skittered into the sun, a long, scuzzy tail wagging just the tiniest bit. It was beyond thin, and even through the caked-on mud and leaves, she could see its ribs.

"Stay here," she said, slowly backing away toward the house. Once she was through the pool cage and fence gate, she hurried into the kitchen and grabbed a plain doughnut. It wasn't dog food, but at least it wasn't chocolate. And this dog didn't look picky.

"Having fun exploring?" her mom asked from the horrifying depths of the ancient fridge.

Lily wasn't about to tell her what was really happening outside, so she just said, "It'd be more fun if the pool wasn't green."

She ran back out before her mom could give a speech about being grateful for what you have, even when what you have is gross.

Outside, the dog-thing waited, tail fluttering cautiously.

As she approached, speaking in a soft voice, it danced toward her and bolted back toward the safety of the shadows, trembling with hope and also probably terror as she held out the doughnut. Finally, the dog crept over on its belly, close enough to snatch up the bit of doughnut she'd tossed to the ground.

Lily squatted down and fed him little bites, talking calmly all the while. He inched closer, tail tucked, but quivering desperately to be near her. Reaching out a tentative hand, she patted the dog's head. At first, he yelped and drew away, but then, unable to stop himself, he belly-crawled back to her and lowered his head, accepting her touch. By the time the doughnut was gone, the dog was by her side, and she could see the shape of him. He seemed like some sort of mutt, one of those bigger dogs mixed with a poodle, but his hair had grown out badly without any care. His ears and tail were long, and his fur was matted with dirt and briars. As she stroked his back and murmured to him, he shivered with pleasure and showed her his belly.

When she scratched around the dog's neck, much to her surprise, she found a collar there.

"What's this, huh, buddy?" she asked, sliding the collar around so she could catch the tags dangling from it. If it were her dog that was lost, she would want someone to check. He was clearly having a bad time of it.

MINE

The tag said the dog's name *actually was* Buddy.

And the address printed on the back was familiar—because it was hers, too.

Buddy had once belonged to the people who lived here before Lily.

5.

RUNNING HER FINGERS AROUND THE COLLAR, LILY UNBUCKLED IT AND pulled it away. It had once been fluorescent orange, maybe, and the tags were all dinged up. Buddy seemed happy to be rid of it and gave his neck a vigorous scratch.

"Let's go show this to Mom," Lily told him. But when she stood up, he bolted back into the undergrowth. With the collar in her hand, she had no way to pull him along, and no matter how sweetly she called him, he seemed unwilling to budge from the safety of the shadows again.

"I'll be back," she promised.

Heading into the house, she found her mom still scrubbing out the fridge and looking miserable.

"I found a dog," Lily said, holding out the collar.

Her mom's nose wrinkled up. "No dogs. You know that."

"But he used to live here. See? This is our address."

Her mom looked down, briefly, and shrugged. "We should probably call animal control. Your father bought the house from the bank, so the old man who lived here must've . . . uh, left him behind. I can't believe anyone would live like this! Just look at it!"

They both glanced around the kitchen. Mounds of trash were everywhere, mostly gunky plastic bowls and trays from instant dinners. Even the milk was the shelf-stable kind that came in boxes. Her mom had made some progress bagging it all, but there was just so much. Everything in the fridge had rotted to a black mush that had apparently decided to climb up every interior surface.

But then Lily realized what her mom had just said. "It wasn't just an old man. There was a little girl who lived upstairs, too."

Her mom cocked her head. "That's not what . . . I don't think that's true. Maybe grandkids came to visit sometimes."

"Her clothes were in the drawers."

Mom nodded like that made sense. "Sure. When you were little, you had a whole dresser of your clothes at Nana's house, too."

"No, it's not like that. It wasn't a guest bedroom. She really did live here. She had a pet snake."

Lily's voice rose with every sentence, and her mom turned to look at her, hands on her hips.

"You don't need to get all riled up. What matters is that it's ours now. So let's use that energy to clean instead of arguing over what's done."

"It's not arguing. I'm just telling you that you're wrong."

Mom sighed. "Lily, please."

Lily gave her own full-body sigh of annoyance. "Okay, fine. I'm wrong and everything here is *totally normal*."

She just stood there for a few moments, eyebrows up, watching her mother struggle to respond, finally settling for the usual—ignoring Lily's thoughts and feelings to talk about things that didn't matter.

"Whoever lived here didn't leave the house much," her mom said with forced cheerfulness. "There wasn't anything fresh in the fridge. No veggies or fruit or eggs. I weep for their colons."

Lily picked up an empty box of Pop-Tarts—the kind that didn't have frosting. "Even their junk food wasn't the good kind of junk food. They had terrible taste." She realized her shoe was stuck to the ground and lifted it with an awful squelchy noise. "Can't you call a house cleaner or something?"

"I tried, before the move. The quote was three times higher once they saw the place, and your dad . . ." Mom snorted, attacking the fridge with a vengeance. "It's not a possibility. But it'll be okay. It's only dirt. And we only have to do it once."

Mom went back to scrubbing without another word about the dog, and Lily put the collar in a junk drawer and went back to bagging garbage. Not that she could forget about poor Buddy, out there all alone . . . But it was going to be hard to sneak him food until they *had* more food. At least he had plenty of water, even if the lake was entirely unsanitary. It hurt her heart, though, to think about how long he'd been living this way, hanging around a house where no one ever came home.

When she got bored with hefting black garbage bags, she started carrying out stacks of empty cans and plastic bottles, grateful each time a little square of counter was revealed. It made her nervous, being in a house where you couldn't quite see the floors or corners. Anything could be hiding under the piles of garbage—rats, spiders, more of those huge roaches. As much as she didn't want to spend her summer break cleaning, she felt a little less weighed down with every bit of trash that left the house. She would definitely breathe better when everything was cleared out. It was like Mom said—they only had to do this once. And being helpful was proof that she was trying to meet her parents halfway.

That night, Dad was in a good mood after his first day at the new job, and they celebrated with fast food—eaten in the restaurant, because the kitchen table was still buried. Mom, as usual, acted chipper and didn't mention how gross their day had been, and Dad was pleased to see their progress. Lily pretended that everything was fine, because that was easier than telling her dad about the freaky things she'd seen and having him loudly accuse her of being overly dramatic again. On the way from the car to the house, she carefully let the leftover half of her bacon cheeseburger drop on the ground where she hoped Buddy would find it.

Well after her usual bedtime, Lily settled into the bed that now felt a little more like her own. She'd moved it to a different wall and made it up nicely with the mattress protector and sheets Mom had dug out of the car, grateful that they still smelled like her old room. She'd covered the drawers in pretty purple shelf paper and filled them with the clothes stuffed in her backpack. She liked the art on the walls well enough, especially the llama, and her old comforter from home went okay with the decor, thanks to a tiny streak of yellow. It was starting to feel like her own place.

She was reading one of the books she'd found on Britney's shelf and was lost in the story when she heard a mournful howl that sent prickles up her spine.

It was probably the dog—Buddy—but it sounded so close and loud and creepy. When she looked out her window, she saw a shadowy lump sitting on the dock. The moon was reflected in the dark water, and the forest rustled as if it were alive. She put a hand to the window glass and felt the summer heat seep into her palm.

Poor Buddy. He seemed so sad. Her plan was to clean him up and then convince her mom to bring him inside, but it was going to take a little time to get him to that stage. It was awful how those people had left him behind like just another piece of their trash. She thought about going outside with some more food and kind words, but . . . it was just plain spooky out there at night, all overgrown and wild and shadowy. And the outside light didn't work sometimes. But she wasn't going to be able to sleep until she'd helped him.

Lily crept downstairs and stopped. The den was still a labyrinth of garbage, even though the piles were diminishing. It looked like a city of forgotten things, and each tower of boxes cast strange shadows in the scant light emanating from the bathroom. But why was the light even on in the downstairs bathroom?

"Mom?" Lily called.

A faint rustle answered her, soft as socks on dusty wood.

"Are you up?"

Another rustle.

Well, her mom kept weird nurses' hours and often stayed up at night listening to life-hacking podcasts on her phone with her earbuds, so maybe she was up cleaning or crocheting and had left the light on to make it easier to see.

Lily stepped off the bottom stair onto the floorboards and instantly wanted to snatch her bare foot back. What if something was hiding down here in the garbage? Sure, it seemed fine during the day, but they'd found rat poop and chewed cardboard lying around, and if there was one giant roach, there had to be a million. She wound her way around stacks of junk and black bags toward the source of the light, holding her breath and trying not to touch anything.

But when she stood in the doorway, there was no sign of her mom. The bathroom was clean now, and the old magazines and grody comb were gone. This would be Lily's bathroom, Mom had said, since her parents had their own bathroom in the master bedroom and she didn't have one upstairs. She hated the old-fashioned pink wallpaper, and it was just plain weird having carpet in a bathroom, but at least she'd gotten to pick out the shower curtain, which was white with cute succulents and cacti on it. When she'd been down here earlier, the shower curtain had been open, showing off a fresh bar of soap and new bottles of shampoo and conditioner and a towel that still had tags. Now the shower curtain was closed.

And when the rustling came again, it came from the bathtub.

Definitely not her mom.

Lily picked up the new toilet brush and tried to control her wildly beating heart. That noise—it was probably a roach, or maybe a trapped moth. Florida was full of supersized bugs. Or maybe it was a cute little mouse.

Her fingers trembled as she reached for the shower curtain and pulled it back with a sudden clank.

The tub was empty.

Not even a teeny spider.

Her arm holding the toilet brush fell to her side.

"Ha. Very funny," she told herself. "I'm soooo melodramatic."

As if in answer, water suddenly gushed out of the tub faucet. It wasn't clean, clear water or even the brown grunge of old pipes. This water was thick and green and viscous, as dark and gooey as the glop in the bottom of the pool outside. Or the swamp.

Lily reached out, trying to close the tap, but it wouldn't budge.

A loud burble behind her made her spin around, and she saw that the toilet was overflowing with the same thick green-black sludge. It rose and rose and flooded over the seat, splattering onto the carpet and soaking it, leaving ink-black stains. The scent of rot and death filled the room, choking her.

"Mom!" she cried. "Mom, help!"

There wasn't a toilet plunger, but it's not like that could've stopped the river of slime seeping into the room. It spread out and soaked into the beige carpet, and she stepped back only to find the bathtub also overflowing. Her heart was beating like crazy, her hair on end and her limbs all numb. She didn't have to act at all—this was real terror.

Her mom didn't show up, and the flooding wouldn't stop, and it was almost touching her toes, despite the fact that she kept backing up and backing up toward the door. She looked around wildly for anything to stop the overflow, but even the sink was oozing now. And written on the recently cleaned mirror in green-black gunk was a single word: *MINE*.

With a loud slam, the bathroom door closed, and the light went out, leaving Lily in total darkness. The thick, warm water squelched between her toes, and it felt like she was sinking in mud, being sucked down into endless depths. She closed her eyes and screamed bloody murder, hard enough to shred her throat, and she felt water touch her face as if the goo was dripping off the ceiling, too.

"Lily?"

She opened her eyes and found her mom staring at her like she'd grown another head. The bathroom light was on, the door was open, and . . . there wasn't a single drop of green-black sludge in sight. The toilet was sparkling clean, the shower curtain was drawn back, and the word scrawled on the mirror was gone.

"Are you okay?" her mom asked, looking utterly exhausted and done. "Why were you screaming? And why are you holding a toilet brush?"

Lily looked around, breathing hard like she'd just run a mile.

What . . . had just happened? She had seen that thick black water. She'd *smelled* it.

Was she sleepwalking? Did she have a fever?

When that grapefruit landed on her head, had she gotten a concussion?

Her mom was waiting for an answer, and . . .

"Uh, there was a roach," she lied. "It surprised me."

Her mother plucked the toilet brush from her hand and shoved it back into its holder. "Yeah, I saw one, too. We've just got to get used to it. It's basically Jurassic Park around here." She put a hand on Lily's shoulder and attempted a tired smile. "I know it's hard, but we can make this work."

"Uh, sure," Lily mumbled, feeling her whole face go red. "Sorry."

"Go back to bed, sweetie. We've got a lot of work to do tomorrow."

Lily nodded. Her throat was all closed up—words wouldn't come. Her mom was waiting, eyebrows raised, so she hurried past her and made a beeline for the stairs. Running up to her room as if she were being chased, she tried to think of a single scenario that could explain what had just happened.

But when she got to her room, she skidded to a halt.

Nothing could explain what she saw.

Her clothes were out of their drawers, tossed everywhere. Her books—not the ones from the shelves, but the only ones she'd brought from Colorado—were lying on the ground like broken birds, their spines snapped. The bed was back in its original place, and Lily's sheets and comforter and pillow were crumpled on the floor like someone had stomped on them. Written on the white mattress again in even bigger ash-gray letters was that same, threatening word.

MINE.

And under that, two more:

GO AWAY.

6.

LILY WANTED TO SCREAM AND SHE WANTED TO RUN AWAY, BUT SHE knew that making a big scene would only make her parents angry. She whipped out her phone and took pics of the mess and the words before hurrying downstairs to her parents' bedroom. The door was closed, and she could hear their voices on the other side. They weren't shouting, but they didn't sound happy.

Well, too bad. Lily wasn't happy, either.

She knocked politely on the door, and her parents' voices went silent. She was bouncing on her toes now, full of energy and scared and excited, but she closed her eyes and shoved the feelings down like a wave smoothing over scribbles in the sand. She had to be calm and reasonable if she wanted them to take her seriously.

The door opened to show her father's glare. "Another roach?"

Lily held out her phone, showing the picture she'd snapped. "I'm sorry to bother you, but someone's been in my room. They messed up all my stuff and wrote on the mattress."

Instead of looking at her phone, he looked past her, down the dark hall, and shook his head. "Lily, I don't know what to say. All the talks we've had since that night, all your apologies, your promises to change. They don't mean anything, do they?"

Lily flinched and shook her head. He had it all wrong.

"No, this isn't me being dramatic. I swear. Just . . . come see." She turned and headed for the stairs. When he didn't immediately follow, she stopped. And stared.

Her father was standing in the door in his robe and pajama pants, looking at her like she'd betrayed him. He turned to glance back at where Mom sat in the bed. "Laura, I can't. I just can't anymore."

He went back into the room, and Lily's mom slid out the door instead.

"Is he not coming?"

Mom looked at the phone, frowning, before putting a hand on her shoulder to steer her away. "Your dad had a long day. Let's go see what's up."

Lily led the way upstairs feeling unsure. Yeah, she regretted what had happened back in Colorado, and she'd said her apologies and begged for forgiveness and promised to be better. But that didn't change what had happened in her room here, now.

Her dad should've definitely cared if some weirdo was sneaking into his house. She'd done what he asked, hadn't been dramatic at all, and he still didn't believe her.

At least Mom was on her side.

But when Mom saw her room, she didn't gasp and rush inside or draw Lily into a comforting hug. She sighed heavily and leaned against the doorframe like she couldn't hold herself up anymore and said, "Really, Lily?"

Lily looked all over the room, trying to figure out what she was missing. "What do you mean?"

"I know you're not getting as much attention as you'd like, and we all know you wanted to stay in Boulder, but . . . acting out like this? Did you think we'd just turn around and go back because you trashed your room and turned it into some fake mystery?" She rubbed her temples and subtly wiped away tears. "It doesn't work, okay? All the drama. It's never going to do what you want it to. Now, put it back together and go to sleep."

But Lily moved to block her mom. She had to make her understand.

"I didn't do this. I wouldn't. That would be stupid. Someone else did it. Maybe—"

"Don't. Just don't. I'm too tired for this."

Her mom stepped around her and left, leaving Lily alone with the mess she definitely hadn't made. Before, she'd felt confused and targeted and uncomfortable, but now she felt utterly abandoned.

They didn't believe her.

Not her dad—no big surprise. And not her mom, either.

Her mom used to be her biggest fan, always, but . . . Well, Lily had watched her parents argue more and more as her dad struggled to find work and didn't, and then their savings dwindled and they sold his much nicer car. As her dad got angrier, her mother seemed to fade away. She just disappeared into her phone or her yarn bag. And sometimes she looked at Lily like it was all her fault.

And now her room—they thought she'd done this *for attention.*

It would've been insulting if it hadn't been so devastating.

Her parents had always told her they were on her side, even when they complained that she was being melodramatic or silly, but now, when she needed them most—*really* needed them—it was clear that they didn't care.

Her eyes went hot and red, and she dashed the tears away with the back of her hand. She wanted to close her eyes and make it all disappear, but every time she tried, she saw the greenish-black water again, saw the word *MINE* scrawled on the mirror. The same word scrawled on the mattress. Again.

Plus the new addition: *GO AWAY.*

Ha. Like she could.

Like that wasn't what she wanted more than anything in the world.

Like she wasn't stuck here, in this gross house, in this crazy room where someone was sneaking in to play some weird prank on her. She wasn't ready to consider any other possibilities.

No way was she going to sleep in that bed. She made a nest on the floor and wrapped her comforter around herself, inhaling the scent of their old house and the familiar tang of Mom's favorite detergent. She was crying, and there were too many reasons why to count. It stung that her dad couldn't even be bothered to leave the room and that her mom had offered her no comfort. And it really hurt, the way they'd both looked at her like she'd betrayed them.

They'd had a big talk before moving down here, everyone seated around the dining room table, and Dad had given her a hard look that made her want to curl up and die. He'd reminded her that this was her chance at a do-over, a chance to make up for her past mistakes and toe the line. Her chance to really look at who she wanted to be and make a lasting change for the better, for her and for the family.

"No drama," he'd said, harsh as a door slamming shut.

"No drama," she'd repeated, her voice small. With those two words, he wasn't just shutting down a behavior but pretty much everything about who she was. That night, she'd stuffed a garbage bag with her most flamboyant and costumey pieces of clothing, her glitter-star sunglasses and unicorn-horn head-band and blue sequined fedora and hot-pink faux-fur jacket. She was really going to try, even if it meant making herself seem smaller.

Even if that felt wrong.

But it hadn't lasted, of course. A leopard couldn't just change her spots.

The drama was just a part of her, and it crept back in like an understudy slinking around backstage, waiting for the chance to shine. But what was happening here went beyond show-ing up to family dinner in head-to-toe rhinestones and stage makeup or singing "Memory" at full volume to every cat she met in an alley. This was real, and yet her parents didn't be-lieve her.

Lily got up and held out her phone, walking around the room and hoping for just one bar. She hadn't had any service since they'd arrived. If she could just talk to CJ, maybe he'd believe her. Finally, in the corner, she found it: one tiny bar. But CJ hadn't sent her a single text today. The last one was from their first night on the road from Colorado. Lily had complained about the cramped car, the increasing heat, and the suck fest of road food, and CJ had responded with GIFs of doughnuts.

New place is the worst, she typed. *Hoarder house! Oodles of garbage! Dead snake in my room! Florida is the armpit of the world! IT'S A HARD KNOCK LIFE FOR US.*

She hit Send and waited. Boulder was two time zones away, so there was a good chance CJ was still up and might answer. It took a few moments, but the response came . . . and wasn't like CJ at all.

GO AWAY THEN it said in all caps, which was weird.

Uh, I can't drive yet and sorta have to do what my parents make me? she responded.

YOU'RE NOT WANTED was the response.

Oooookay, she texted back. *I expected GIFs of alligators, but you're being mean.*

The answer took longer this time but was just as puzzling.

JUST LEAVE JUST GO THIS ISN'T YOUR HOME

All caps, really? And did you forget punctuation? she shot back, because CJ was, among other things, a grammar nerd.

IT WAS ALL MINE AND I WANT IT BACK

And then the phone rang in her hand. She pulled away and stared at it; nobody actually talked on their phones! And the call wasn't from CJ's number—the phone said *Unknown Caller.* Lily thumbed the volume down so her parents wouldn't freak out and watched the phone ring and ring and ring. Voice mail should've picked up, but it didn't. It just kept ringing.

Finally she answered it.

"You're being a real butt, you know," she barked.

But the only answer was creepy breathing.

And that's when she realized it wasn't CJ.

Her body went rigid, like she'd been struck by lightning, her hairline going hot and her teeth grinding as her hands shook.

"Who is this?" she whispered.

"Go away," a little girl's voice said. "Unless you want to play."

"No!" Lily shouted back, furious and terrified. "I'm not going anywhere. *You* go away!"

The voice laughed and laughed, mad and high-pitched.

Then the phone went dead.

7.

LILY STARED AT THE PHONE IN HER HAND. WHAT HAD JUST HAPPENED?

She went to turn it back on, but the second her finger touched the power button, a real spider skittered across the screen. With a gasp, she threw the phone across the room, where it hit the wall and clattered to the ground. She danced around, slapping at herself, but she couldn't find the spider again, so she walked over and stared down at where her phone had fallen. The screen was black now and webbed with cracks, but she remembered the words she'd seen there.

GO AWAY.

THIS ISN'T YOUR HOME.

MINE.

Those same words again.

The only answer that made sense was . . . Britney. Maybe she'd moved out but still lived nearby. Maybe she'd been sneaking in to mess with . . . well, the new girl taking over her old room. Maybe she'd written on the mattress, moved the bed, messed with the books—as revenge. It had only been Lily's things that had been messed with, after all. Maybe Britney had been waiting for someone to unlock the house so she could get her stuff, and instead, Lily had thrown all her stuff in the dumpster, buried it under a ton of garbage.

That had to be it.

"Lily?"

She spun around to find her mother standing in the doorway looking even more exhausted and angry than before. "Did you just throw something? We heard it from downstairs."

"There was a spider. I—"

Her mom waved that away and walked across the room, picking up her phone and examining the new cracks in the glass with a frown.

"Having your own phone is a big responsibility," she began. "You know how tight money is."

Lily's whole body felt like a fist. "Yeah, I know. We can't even afford a crappy cleaning service."

"Lily—"

"There. Was. Almost. A. Spider. On. My. Hand."

"The solution to that problem is not throwing an expensive piece of technology across the room. I'm just going to take this with me. Maybe in a week, if you can stop all this over-the-top, attention-seeking nonsense, we can talk about returning it."

"But, Mom—"

"No." Her mom stared at her, eyes wet, cheeks red, lips pursed, pushed to the edge in a way that Lily had seen only once before. "No. It stops now. No more. I don't want to come up here again. Go to bed."

She left with the phone, and Lily deflated. How could the situation have gotten even worse? Now she had no phone. No way to contact CJ. No way to look at those crazy messages and reassure herself that she wasn't making it all up.

There wasn't much else to do. Her parents were clearly awake and furious with her, and they'd told her repeatedly to go to bed. She checked every corner of her room and locked the door in case Britney or whoever tried to come in while she was sleeping. She curled up in the little nest she'd made on the floor, feeling the raw wood boards press, cruel and unyielding, against her bones. She thought she might be awake for the rest of her life after everything that had happened, but she somehow fell asleep after midnight.

The next morning, she remade the bed with her mattress cover and sheets and comforter and pushed it laboriously back to where she liked it. If someone wanted to mess with her, she would mess right back with them. As more and more of the house got cleared out, there would be fewer places for some creepy kid to hide and write on things. Which meant that Lily was going to get to work and double her efforts.

She put on a sleep tank and a pair of jeans recently snipped into cutoffs and stomped downstairs. Her mom had apparently gotten up early, and she'd made lots of progress on the den while Lily slept. The heavy white curtains, thankfully, were gone, and light shone brightly through a wall made entirely of dirty windows. Lily could see the furniture now—squishy tan couches and another big, worn leather recliner. The TV was older, though, the kind that was more like a cube. The newspapers and most of the bags were gone, but half of the room was still stacked to the ceiling with Amazon boxes. Her mom marched in the door looking determined and furious, but she softened just a little when she saw Lily.

"Are we going to have any problems today?" she asked.

Lily sighed and felt the full weight of every accusation pressing down on her. "No. What do you want me to do?"

Her mom put her hands on her hips and looked around. "If you can begin in the laundry room, maybe we can start washing things. Jack said the washer and dryer worked."

Lily hadn't seen the laundry room yet, but her mom led her there, stopping in the kitchen for the requisite yellow gloves, trash bags, paper towels, and heavy-duty cleaner. The house was put together strangely, with all sorts of odd angles, and Lily realized that there was still a lot to discover.

Her mom left her in a room with industrial shelves still covered with open boxes of nonperishable food. She couldn't see much of the floor, and she had to assume that the lumpy shapes hidden by mountains of dirty clothes were the washer and dryer. Something smelled utterly horrific, and she wasn't sure if it was mildewed clothes, rotten food, or something worse. There was a door to the outside, too, and her first goal was to work her way over to it and open it for some fresh—if meltingly hot—air. And to toss a chunk of stale doughnut out for Buddy.

Time seemed to fade away as Lily stuffed stiffened clothes into black garbage bags and hauled them out to the dumpster. Her shoulders and back were sore from all of yesterday's work, but at least the little aches and pains helped take her mind off last night as she worked. Unlike Britney's clothes upstairs, the garments in the laundry room weren't clean or tidy. They were heavy with stains that were dried and weathered into strange shapes.

Lily was starting to get a picture of who had lived here most recently, the person who had left such a disgusting mess behind: the old man her mom had mentioned. There were overalls, ugly pleated pants, and hundreds of yellowed white undershirts. Everything reeked of body odor and cologne. Every time she found a pair of plaid boxer shorts, she was grateful for her gloves. The butter-gold sun beat down through the broken blinds, and sweat trickled down her neck and into her eyes. It was like living in a fever, like breathing soup. Finally, the washer and dryer were revealed, not that they were particularly exciting.

Lily stuffed the last layer of clothes into a full-to-bursting bag and turned to go and let her mom know that she'd followed directions without causing trouble—and that she'd succeeded. But then something caught her eye. A sinister shape sidled out from the dark crack between the dusty white machines. Lily jumped back, her leg pressing against the garbage bag.

It was a spider—the big, hairy, skittery kind.

Little spiders she could deal with. Orb weavers were kinda cool. She'd held a tarantula once, even. And the spider last night, the one that had made her throw the phone—in retrospect, it was teeny. But this was a wolf spider the size of her hand, and it was crawling right at her.

Lily spun around to grab something from the shelf to kill it with, a cobwebbed box of ramen or two-liter bottle of soda. But as she reached toward the shelf, another spider burst out from behind an old cereal box.

The back of her neck itched, and she swatted at it, but there was nothing there. Tiny tickles ran up the back of her calf. A giant spider waited by the light switch, fangs reaching for her fingers. They were everywhere, squeezing out of cracks in the wood and out from behind the washer and out of the black bag she'd been packing with clothes. Hundreds of spiders, brown and gold and black with red hourglasses, pincers working busily, legs softly scurrying. She was frozen in place, numb, as if her body had forgotten how to move. They were on every surface, all of them moving at once, swiftly, right at her.

With a strangled gulp, Lily leapt over the bag and ran back into the kitchen. She spun around, expecting to find spiders here, too. She must've broken open a nest somewhere, among all those nasty old clothes. But the kitchen was mostly normal, and she didn't see a single furry brown body. She snatched a spatula from the mason jar by the old stove and tiptoed toward the laundry room, ready to start smacking. But when she peeked inside . . . the spiders were gone.

Seriously. She couldn't see a single spider at all, not even a scrap of web.

It made no sense. Not only the weird things that kept happening, but the way she kept seeing things that weren't there. Yes, she was dramatic, and yes, she had a big imagination, but the Florida heat had to be melting her brain.

She wanted to tell her mom, but the spiders, like the gushing swamp water in the bathroom, were completely gone. Not that having actual evidence had changed anyone's mind in her room last night. If she told her mom she was seeing thousands of spiders, it would just be one more dramatic rebellion, one more reason to assume she was going to continue being a problem. Or worse, her mom might think she was legit going crazy.

No, she had to deal with this on her own.

Creeping back into the laundry room, she kicked the black garbage bag full of clothes, but nothing happened. So she hooked her spatula through the pull ties and dragged the bag into the kitchen and out to the dumpster without touching it.

Her mom could toss it in later. When she stepped into the laundry room again, she felt twitchy and cold, as if a thousand—well, if they were spiders, eight thousand—tiny eyes watched her from the shadows. But she didn't see a single arachnid or bug, not even a mosquito, which were everywhere. Lily's breathing was still more like panting, and she began to wonder what it was called when you just panicked all the time—for real—and never stopped.

The only antidote to being freaked out by invisible nonsense was to throw herself into work. She was super jumpy as she opened a new garbage bag and began tipping the leftover food from the shelves into it. Bulk boxes of ramen noodles, canisters of drink powder, unopened boxes of breakfast tarts, giant boxes of fiber cereal, and flats of potato chips used up ten more big black garbage bags. It took all her strength to lug the bags outside and line them up by the dumpster, but within a few hours, she had the laundry room all but empty. There was nowhere left for spiders to hide—not that she found any evidence that there had even been spiders.

The last thing she did was fetch the broom and sweep all the dusty crevices. In part because she knew that if she didn't do it, her mom would just ask her to, and in part to make absolutely sure there were no places where an entire nest of spiders could be hiding. When she shoved the broom in the crevice between the washer and dryer, the bristles scraped over something bigger than the usual dust bunnies.

Lily refused to stick her hand in there, so she used the broom to pry it out. It was a sheaf of yellowed papers carefully clipped together. Unfilled prescriptions from the hospital three years ago. All for a man named Brian Richardson.

There were six different ones, all dated on the same day and signed by the doctor in pen. Lily didn't know what everything was, but since her mom was a nurse, she recognized antibiotics and heart medicine. Brian—that must've been the old man. And he definitely had not been healthy. But if he'd bothered to go to the hospital, why hadn't he filled his prescriptions? Or changed his horrible eating habits, which seemed to be mostly things that came in boxes? She realized that he had once stood here, holding this same sheaf of papers. The thought made her shiver.

A little girl's room left untouched and an old man with a hoarding problem who didn't take care of himself. Oh! And a dog, Buddy, left behind.

Nothing about this place made sense.

There was something else going on, something she couldn't quite see.

All she knew was that she was stuck here, with whatever wouldn't leave her alone.

8.

IN THE END, LILY TOSSED THE PRESCRIPTIONS IN THE TRASH. SHE sprayed and scrubbed the laundry room shelves and cleaned the dusty window until the whole room sparkled. Maybe if they could get the house empty enough and clean enough, it would just be . . . normal.

As she rubbed the last streaks off the window, the glistening water of the lake outside caught her eye. The afternoon was oppressively hot, but the view was pretty, with sunbeams slanting through the forest and dappled shadows dancing over the water. She hadn't explored this side of the house yet—the swamp side. She'd done what her mother had asked her to do, so she decided she could take a little time off to poke around the yard.

She stripped off her filthy gloves and chucked them in the last garbage bag. Mom had already taken two carloads of donations to the secondhand store, but it turned out that most of the stuff here was actual trash. Apparently, the previous owners had just stopped taking the can outside and left everything where it fell.

When Lily shouldered open the laundry room door and stepped outside, she felt like she suddenly weighed less, like she'd been carrying rocks and was now light and free. Her mom had bought her a cheap pair of flip-flops on one of her store runs, and Lily didn't want to ruin her much nicer sneakers, so she slipped on the flops to go exploring—and look for clues.

The gravel path from the laundry room door led around to the lake. It was shadier here, and empty bird feeders and broken mobiles dangled from the tree branches, swaying in the hot puffs of . . . well, it wasn't a breeze. It was more like the lake was breathing, the air steamy and moist and heavy. Tiny flowers dotted the path, and as Lily neared the shade of the trees, the ground squelched under her feet. This side of the lake was apparently as swampy as it looked. She stepped under the trees and scanned between the heavy trunks to see what might be hiding within the forest.

Up ahead, maybe a hundred feet away, the sunlight slanted onto ground as wet as pudding, and strange little plants poked up like straws, or maybe train whistles. Where the sun shone through them, they were lit a lively neon green, and iridescent dragonflies buzzed here and there on glittery wings. Lily realized she was looking at pitcher plants—they'd done a unit on carnivorous plants last year, but she'd never seen them in real life. It was actually pretty cool. Step by step, water sloshing between her toes, she waded into the marsh. Just this one little patch of forest was lit up, almost like a fairy spotlight was shining down. Time seemed to stop, caught like a veined wing in amber, like honey in a jar.

For the first time in what seemed like days, she smiled, remembering when she'd played Mustardseed in the local theater's production of *A Midsummer Night's Dream* and fantasized about stepping in as understudy for the adult playing Puck. Her posture changed, and she was almost skipping.

> *"If we shadows have offended,*
> *Think but this, and all is mended,*
> *That you have but slumber'd here*
> *While these visions did appear.*
> *And this weak and idle theme,*
> *No more yielding but a dream . . ."*

She trailed off. It felt good, slipping back into a fairy's skin, if only for a moment. This was indeed a very puckish place, magical and green and deep. Maybe at least part of Florida wasn't so terrible.

When she was close enough to touch one of the little plants,

Lily ran a finger over its high hat, which snapped down to cover the strawlike end. She jerked her finger back, amused and enchanted. She hadn't known pitcher plants could do that. But when the top slowly opened again and she looked inside, something wasn't right.

It looked like the pitcher plant was full of blood.

Thick scarlet liquid pooled there, a dead fly floating in it. Lily checked the next plant and the next, and each one had some old, dead bug floating in syrupy blood. When she looked down at her hand, it was speckled with bright red drops, thick and wet.

Her stomach turned, and she stepped backward and tripped on a root, landing hard on her butt with a splash. The muddy water soaked into her shorts, cold and clammy, and she bolted up and turned to hurry home. But where was her house? All she could see was more of the same boggy forest, thick-rooted trees and drooping branches dangling with curly gray moss. There were no more sunbeams, no more spotlights. The sky seemed to sigh into a soft grayish brown like a hidden bruise inside an apple.

"This isn't right," she said to herself, stumbling ahead in the muck. She couldn't see her house, but she knew it was this way—it had to be. Cold crept down her neck, numbing her fingers.

A sudden movement at her feet made her look down, and she froze.

It was a snake. A big, black, angular thing with a heart-shaped head the size of her fist. She didn't know what type it was, but she knew it was poisonous—no, venomous—and that it was angry. Its neck was drawn back, its slit eyes gleaming. As it struck, Lily jumped away, turned, and ran deeper into the boggy forest.

The swamp all looked the same when you were terrified and running, and Lily just had to hope that she wasn't heading toward deeper water, where gators had to live. She pushed vines and moss out of the way, scrambled over logs, and tripped over roots. Her shorts were soaked with mud, and she lost a flip-flop somewhere in the muck. She reached for the pocket where she usually kept her phone, but it wasn't there. Her mom had taken it last night. All she could do was keep going. Finally, she heard laughter somewhere ahead and stumbled toward it.

Soon she saw shapes through the trees. Green grass, bodies moving, a . . . trampoline? She stepped out of the soggy bog and onto a nice lawn, and two kids stopped jumping on a caged-in trampoline to stare at her.

"Uh, are you lost?" asked the older one, a sporty-looking guy who was maybe fifteen.

"Who are you? Are you new? What are you doing in the swamp?" asked the younger one, a pretty girl about Lily's age. They both had dark skin, and the girl's hair was in long twists.

"What . . . am I doing . . . in your swamp?" Lily said in Shrek's voice, realizing as she heard her wobbling words that it was a pretty stupid thing to say, and a slight misquote, and that maybe she was losing her mind. "I mean . . ." She trailed off. She sounded crazy, and she probably looked terrible. She could feel the sweat matting down her dark hair, the dirt clinging to her mosquito-bitten, blood-flecked hands.

"My name is Lily. I just moved in. I saw a snake and ran," she finally managed, possibly the least dramatic thing she'd ever said.

"Was it poisonous?" the boy asked.

"Venomous," Lily and the girl said at the same time, and they both smiled. And then Lily did the dumbest thing in the world and burst out crying.

These were real tears, and they came out hot and heavy. She covered her face with her hands and wished this was all a bad dream.

The girl jumped off the trampoline and hurried over, putting an arm around Lily with the warm familiarity of someone who was already her friend. "Oh wow, so you're pretty messed up, huh?" the girl asked. "I'm Rachel. That's Kyle. He's a jerk. But whatever. Come inside. You probably need some water, right? You look . . ."

"Gross?" Lily offered between hiccups.

"I was going to say dehydrated."

Rachel steered Lily inside a flawlessly clean pool cage and sat her down on a patio couch. When Lily gestured to her dirty shorts, Rachel gently shook her head and said, "Carla will deal with it. Now, stay put."

Lily looked around, wondering who Carla was. Moments later, Rachel reappeared and put a cold can of soda into Lily's hand. Lily gulped the soda and coughed when the bubbles hit home. Rachel was right—her throat was dry, her tongue swollen. How long had she been out there? The sun was just starting to dip down behind the trees around the lake, strips of red and purple and orange reflected in the clear water. Was that the same lake that she lived on? And where were Rachel's parents?

"So you got lost," Rachel prompted, curling up and tucking her feet under her on the other side of the couch.

"Yeah. We just moved here a few days ago. I was exploring the swamp behind my house, and . . ."

Lily paused. Thanks to her parents, there was now a block in her head, this little voice urging her to *just be normal, cut the theatrics, don't make everything such a big deal.*

But they weren't here, and Lily was still Lily, so she launched into a full description of what had happened, with hand gestures, tiptoeing like Puck, leaping back from the snake. She didn't say the pitcher plants were full of blood, she said they *looked like* they were full of blood, but otherwise, the story didn't change. Sure, she might've pumped it up just a little bit for effect, but in her defense, Rachel was as rapt as a kid in the front row of their favorite play.

"Ohmygod," Rachel said, all in a rush, her eyes lit up. "That was amazing! You're so good. Are you an actor? Is all that true? Because wow."

Lily felt a gooey loosening in her chest, that warm glow that suffused her anytime someone praised her performance. "Yeah, acting is kind of my thing. And it's mostly true. But seriously, I have no idea where I am."

"The lake is huge," Rachel agreed. "Lake Silence. It's part swamp, part lake, and super deep in the middle. They can't even measure how deep. Like, it used to be one of those crazy sinkholes."

"Sinkholes? Wait, I read about those. They're one of the many ways to die here."

Instead of drawing back like that was an odd thing to say, Rachel leaned forward. "I know, right? Did you know this part of Florida is the sinkhole capital of the world? Something about ancient limestone and the water table, blah blah blah science, and sometimes the ground just opens up and swallows stuff. Even cars and houses and people. It's crazy."

Lily felt cold down to her toes and wished she could ask for a towel. But any towels at this house would probably be solid white and very expensive. She recovered quickly, hoping Rachel wouldn't pick up on her weirdness.

"That's pretty crazy," she echoed. "So . . . where are we? Like, what's your address? My house is on Old Oak Grove."

Rachel nodded excitedly, but then, everything seemed to excite her. "Yeah, our neighborhood is just off that. I can get you home, no problem. Wanna take the boat?"

Lily looked out at the water. It was still as glass, reflecting the sunset and a patch of tall cattails and water lilies.

"If we hurry. I mean, it's about to get dark. Or Carla could drive you," Rachel added. She frowned. "She's getting old, though, and her eyes are bad at night."

"Who's Carla?"

Rachel's frown deepened. "She's kinda like a housekeeper and nanny? She's supposed to watch us when both of my parents are at work or out of town, which is always, but she mostly just watches reality TV and eats cookies these days."

Lily did not want to explain herself to an adult right now, or have Rachel see the mess around the dumpster and make snap judgments.

"Oh, then the boat sounds good."

Rachel hopped up, hurried inside, and returned clutching a key ring attached to a foam alligator. "No problem. I love taking the boat out. Kyle's bored to death of it, but I never have anyone to hang with. You okay now?"

Lily looked down. She'd slurped up the entire soda and snarfed down several cookies, and she did feel a lot better. "Yeah, I'm good. I look like a drowned rat, though."

Rachel shrugged. "Florida hair, don't care—right?"

Lily did care, but she wasn't about to mention that part. She followed Rachel past the trampoline, where Kyle was lying on his back, playing a game on his phone.

"Come back soon, Swamp Thing," he called out.

"Ignore him," Rachel told her. "He's really not that bad. And she was quoting *Shrek*, you jerk."

Rachel's dock was fresh and clean, and there was a tidy metal building attached to it. She used one of her keys to unlock the door, and inside was a small boat with an engine off the back. Soon they were zooming into the middle of the lake. Remembering what Rachel had said about how deep it was, Lily clutched her seat and looked around for a life jacket, but she didn't see anything that looked remotely capable of saving her from drowning.

"Life jacket?" she asked.

"It's Florida," Rachel said. "Everybody has a pool. You can swim, right?"

"Not well."

Rachel grimaced and slowed the boat down. "Sorry. I should've asked. So I guess you came from somewhere far away, then, huh?"

"Colorado."

"Hey, mountains!"

"Yeah, we have those."

"So why are you here?"

Normally, Lily would've launched into another monologue about her woes, but . . . well, the circumstances of her moving were too embarrassing, and most of what had happened at the new house would just scare Rachel away.

"My dad got a new job. Our stuff isn't even here yet. And our house belonged to hoarders. It's a whole thing."

"That sucks."

Just hearing it acknowledged flooded Lily's heart with relief. "Yeah, it does."

"Let me know when you see your house, by the way. Does anything look familiar?"

They were out in the middle of the lake now, and Lily could see all the houses ringing the shore. But these houses looked way more expensive than her own—they all looked like little castles. She spotted a wild tangle of woods that stood out from the manicured lawns. "Maybe over there? It's not so fancy. Or pretty. It's not in a neighborhood, and it's kinda swampy and old by my house."

Rachel steered the boat in the direction Lily had indicated. The water was less smooth here and more . . . well, not lumpy, exactly. But there were yellow reeds and carpets of green lilies clogging the way. Finally, Lily spotted the jagged angles of her brown house hidden under the trees.

"There it is. The . . . uh, weird brown one."

Rachel sat forward a little. "Oh cool! I've never been over

here before. Always kinda wondered what it was, you know? It gets creepy."

"Yeah, it does."

"I don't mean in a bad way," Rachel said, her eyes flying wide with embarrassment. "I mean it's all . . . I don't know. Over where we live, they keep everything so trimmed and maintained. But here, it's like it's *haunted*. Is that your dock?"

Lily could only nod. Rachel's words had struck her like a spotlight. All the weird things that were happening, the strange things she was seeing . . . When she was alone and trapped inside, she wouldn't let herself so much as think about that word, but with Rachel here, looking at her house from a distance, she had to consider it.

If it wasn't Britney sneaking in, was Lily being haunted?

9.

RACHEL DROPPED LILY OFF AT THE WOBBLY LITTLE DOCK, AND LILY PUT
every brain cell she had into not looking like a complete klutz.
After seeing Rachel's, well, *mansion,* she was feeling pretty
self-conscious about her entire deal. Her clothes were old and
dirty, she was currently a total mess, and her house was a disgusting wreck. But Rachel didn't seem to care—she seemed
weirdly curious about Lily's house, staring at it with bright
eyes like she was looking for something in particular. It seemed
like she actually wanted to hang out, too. Of course Lily's mom
still had her phone, so she gave Rachel her number for later.

"I don't get a strong signal here," Lily said. "Would you
want to, I don't know, set up a time to meet? Just in case?"

Rachel's nose scrunched up. "You don't get a signal here?
This place is crawling with signal." She pulled out the latest
phone in a glitter case. "Yeah, see? I have full bars."

"Maybe my phone still thinks it's in Colorado," Lily joked.

"Maybe," Rachel agreed easily. "I have ice skating in the morning, but I can meet you here at three? We can explore the lake."

That, at least, felt hopeful. "Sounds good," Lily said.

Rachel didn't pull away from the dock immediately, and Lily wasn't sure if she was waiting to make sure Lily got inside safely or taking another moment to look around. Hopefully her prospective friend saw it as more magical and interesting than gross and weird.

As the boat finally burbled away and she reached the front door, Lily suddenly realized that she might be in trouble. Her dad would be home, and she'd been gone almost past dark without telling anyone where she was going. It wasn't her fault that she didn't have her phone, but her parents wouldn't want to hear it. Not only that, but she was covered in mud and missing a flip-flop. She stood outside the door catching her breath, but when she turned the knob, it was locked. She knocked, suddenly feeling very alone. She didn't dare look behind her at the darkness of the forest. Rachel's boat was gone. Lily felt like the only person for miles, lost in a wild place.

Knocking at her own door was a peculiar sensation, but it was even stranger to have it swing open and see her father in a suit staring at her like she was a bad salesman interrupting dinner.

"Lily," he said, as if surprised to recall that she existed. "Where have you been? Your mother was worried sick."

"I got a little lost," she started, trying to keep the drama low and sound reasonable and calm. "I was exploring in the backyard and I saw a snake and I ran away and then . . . I was somewhere else."

"Why didn't you call?"

"Mom took my phone."

His frown suggested he knew why. "And did I hear a boat motor?" he asked.

"Yeah." She looked down at her muddy feet. "Rachel drove me back. I ended up . . ." She wasn't sure how to say it, really. "At her mansion?"

Her dad gave a little sigh-snort. "A mansion? Really?"

She huffed a sigh of her own. "Or a McMansion? I don't know what you call it. They had a trampoline and a pool and soft grass and a housekeeper, and Rachel was really nice and drove me home—"

There was this trick her dad pulled—his own kind of drama, although he would never call it that—when he seemed to go from quiet and thoughtful to big and angry, almost like he had finally noticed her and had to expand himself just to deal with her. When he did that, when he took a deep breath and swelled up tall with anger and loomed over her like a bully, she knew she was in trouble. And he was doing it now.

"So you're telling me you ran out into the swamp without even telling your mother you were leaving, and then you played on a trampoline and got in a boat with a stranger?"

His voice was rising, but he didn't seem to know it.

Lily swallowed, her throat gone dry and scratchy. She shrunk down, suddenly aware of how dark it was outside, how prickly her skin felt, how the bits of gravel bruised her one bare foot.

"I guess she was a stranger, but she was my age," Lily said, her voice tiny. "And I wasn't trying to make Mom worry. I told you—she took my phone. I didn't mean to wade into the swamp. There was a snake—a venomous snake—and when it tried to bite me, I just ran."

Dad huffed a big, disappointed sigh. "You know it's hard for me to believe you when I don't know what's true and what you're making up; and your story gets bigger and more unbelievable with every telling." He rubbed his eyes like it hurt to look at her. "Your mom told me about last night. Lily, *we talked about this.*"

"I'm not making up any of it, I swear."

It was a line made for shrieking at full volume, arms waving in the sky, but she delivered it at almost a whisper, her head hanging.

"You keep screaming at every little thing, waking us up over nothing. You broke your phone. You wrecked your room.

You left the house without telling anyone and came back with some stranger. What am I supposed to do? Ground you? Forbid you from doing drama this fall?"

Lily gasped. "Please. Anything but that. I'll be good. Better. Please." He could take away everything else, her life in Colorado and her friends and her phone, but she couldn't deal with the possibility of losing the one thing she loved the most. "I promise."

Her dad sighed and stepped back to let Lily inside. She skulked in, hoping he would just do what he always did and disappear so he wouldn't have to deal with her. They stood there for a moment, saying nothing, and if it had been a play, Lily would've said, "Line?" because she honestly didn't know what should happen next.

"Go get cleaned up," her dad said. "I can't deal with this right now. It's been a long day." He sounded resigned. Not just about the current conflict, but about their entire relationship, in which he just flat out didn't like or approve of who Lily really was.

She started to hang her head again, but then she stuck out her chin stubbornly. She had done nothing wrong. Kids were supposed to explore and play outside, weren't they? And being dramatic wasn't the worst thing to be; it had worked out pretty well for everyone in Hollywood and on Broadway.

But she didn't prolong the fight; she knew she'd already

lost it months ago. She just muttered, "Yes, sir," and went up the stairs to her room.

Everything was just the way she had left it. Lily hadn't realized until then that she had been worried it would be messed up again, with her sheets and books dumped onto the floor and more creepy words written on things. It made her feel strangely powerless, and now, thanks to Rachel's offhand comment about haunting, it also felt like maybe there was something even more terrifying under the surface, something that couldn't be explained away by an angry kid playing pranks.

But Lily could only face one problem at a time, so she might as well do what her dad had told her to do and get cleaned up—which, for once, was what she wanted to do anyway, since she'd recently sat down in an actual swamp. After grabbing a pair of pajamas, she hurried downstairs to the bathroom. She turned on the sink faucet quickly to make sure the water was clear, which it was. The open toilet was clean, too. She wanted to close the bathroom door for privacy, but then again . . . she didn't. Lily didn't like feeling trapped. So she left it open, just a crack.

She turned on the shower and waited until the water was hot, then climbed in. The hot water felt good, but Lily still didn't feel safe. She'd seen something in this bathroom, she'd felt something, some presence. And that word that kept popping up—*MINE*. Whose? Why?

On one hand, she wanted to run away forever and go back home to Colorado. But on the other hand, she was here, and their old house was already sold, and she had no choice. Although she kept hoping that good behavior might mean they could move back, she knew, deep down, that even if she became the perfect, quiet, untroublesome daughter her father craved, she was stuck here. This was where she had to live, this was where she had to shower. This was her bathroom, and this was her house, and this was her life. She wasn't going to skulk around, afraid of angering some random sneaky kid or weird dumb ghost. As Miss Cora had always told the kids with stage fright, "It's okay to be afraid. Everyone is. Feel the fear and do it anyway."

That was one thing Lily could do: Feel the fear and do it anyway.

Even when "it" was something as seemingly simple as taking a shower.

When she was clean, she dried off quickly, got dressed, and went to the laundry room to deposit her dirty clothes. That room, too, was just as she'd left it—empty and as clean as possible, not a spider in sight. The den even looked better, with all the garbage gone except the huge stacks of Amazon boxes looming in the corners and against the walls.

In the kitchen, she found her parents trying to smile over a couple of boxes of still-hot pizza.

"Lots of delivery options around here," her mom said, aiming for perky and falling short. "It's not so uncivilized after all."

"How's work going?" Lily asked her dad as she helped herself to the pizza. The best way back into his good graces was to act cheerful, well-behaved, and interested in whatever he cared about.

"Good," he answered. "Really good." But he didn't go into details. He never did. Lily wasn't even totally sure what he did for a living. Something with data. Something boring he could never quite explain.

They mostly ate in silence after that. Her parents were clearly trying to avoid talking about her and the trouble they thought she'd caused, so Lily didn't say anything, either.

She tried to focus on something positive instead. With the house slowly appearing from under all the looming junk, it seemed like the oppressive pall was lifting. It had been impossible to be happy when they were surrounded by so much trash, so much disorder, the moldering remains of someone else's life that had not gone to plan. Now, for the first time, Lily looked around the kitchen and did not see rot and ruin. She saw clean counters, a nicely swept floor, and little touches that made it feel welcoming. Her mom had chosen bright tropical colors for the kitchen towels, spatulas, and other doodads, a cheerful reminder that maybe Florida wouldn't be so bad after all.

And maybe, eventually, it wouldn't be. They just had to keep making the house feel homey and alive again. Just had to keep clearing out all its tightly held secrets.

Had Lily been imagining all these strange things? After all, she hadn't gotten nearly enough sleep and the move was beyond stressful. She had only ever lived in one place, in that one house in Boulder. Now she was two thousand miles away, in a different time zone, in a different environment. And, well, she wasn't at her best. Her imagination was definitely taking some detours, and the weird climate with its heavy, wet, non-mountainous oxygen wasn't helping.

That night, she tossed some pizza crusts outside for Buddy, checked that the downstairs doors were all locked, and went to sleep before midnight. She had an unusually nice dream about floating in clear blue water under a bright blue sky and woke up feeling slightly less terrible. Back in Colorado her parents had told her that if she really focused on not being so dramatic and applied herself, eventually it would become easier, that faking it would, essentially, help her make it.

Perhaps if she acted as if everything were normal, everything would actually go back to being normal.

Perhaps.

10.

LILY SLEPT SO WELL THAT SHE DIDN'T DREAD COMING DOWNSTAIRS the next morning. If her parents were going to stubbornly pretend nothing had happened, so would she. With the garbage mostly gone, the sun filled the den, making bright and pretty patches of butter yellow on the warm wooden boards. The huge windows showed a gorgeous view of the lake. The couches almost looked comfortable now—almost. They'd seemed moldy and clammy before, squishy enough to sink into, like quicksand. But her mom had done an excellent job cleaning everything the previous owners had left behind. For the first time, Lily smiled as she looked around.

"What are we doing today?" she asked her mom, who was cleaning out the dank cabinet under the kitchen sink.

"Our bedroom needs a lot of work," her mom said. "If you can start on the cardboard boxes in the den, that would be a lot of help. They're too big to fit in the recycling can, so we need to break them down, flatten them, and toss them in the dumpster. I can't believe it, but we're already running out of room in there."

Lily nodded. "If I finish, would it be okay if I went out with Rachel at three o'clock? She's coming to the dock with her boat."

Her mom looked up, brow furrowed. "Is that the girl who brought you home yesterday?"

"Yeah. She lives on the other side of the lake. She seems really nice. Maybe a little lonely."

And then Mom acted exactly like a mom, asking, "Did you meet her parents? Was she reckless when she was driving the boat? I don't know how they do things around here, but it seems a little strange, letting a child drive a boat." And then her eyebrows drew dangerously down. "And while we're at it, what on earth possessed you to wander into the swamp alone yesterday? Your father said something about a snake."

So Lily told her mother the safe and undramatic version of the story, making it clear that most of it wouldn't have happened in the first place if she'd had her phone. She turned it into a simple tale of being lost in a new place, underlining how scared she was and how very much she missed her phone.

She definitely did not mention the lack of life vests in Rachel's boat.

"I met her brother. He's maybe fifteen. He was nice enough. And she seemed like she knew what she was doing. She drove pretty slow."

Her mom was thinking about it. "I'm still upset about your phone, but I can't hold you captive in this crazy old house all summer, so I guess that's fine," she finally said. "You can take your phone with you—just while you're out, not for good— but I want you to be more careful. Don't go too far away and don't take any unnecessary risks. We don't know this place yet. That lake looks deep. And I'm certain this area has reported necrotizing fasciitis and brain-eating amoebas in their water." She stood and pulled Lily's phone out of a drawer and handed it over.

Lily felt a rush of relief—and guilt. The screen was a wreck.

"Consider this a trial run," her mom said in mom voice. "Drop that in the swamp, and you won't get another one for a year. And you won't see Rachel again, either."

"I'll be careful, I promise." The weight of the phone was a comfort in her hand, and there was no way she'd drop it in the swamp. It was her lifeline to CJ and now Rachel, too. "Wait, do you have any bars here?" Lily asked. "I don't. I found one for just a few seconds but . . . well, the texts didn't seem to go through."

Mom pulled her own phone out of her back pocket. "Three bars. Not bad. We may need to look into another carrier. I want to make sure I can always find you."

Lily turned on her phone and was surprised to also see three bars. Maybe there was something about her room that made the signal sketchy. At least now she'd feel a little better exploring outside. Careful not to press too hard on the cracks in the screen, she checked her messages. There were dozens of texts from CJ, and when she was alone again, she would enjoy reading through them and sending back some of their favorite memes in return. But the weird text exchange from the night before was gone.

"Mom, did you erase some of my messages?" she asked.

Her mother looked up in surprise. "Of course not. That would be a betrayal of trust."

Funny, Lily thought, how her mom thought erasing messages was the end of the world when the real betrayal of trust was not believing her daughter when she was telling the truth. Either way, the weird all-caps messages were gone, and nothing could bring them back.

Mom left to work on her bedroom, and after tossing some slices of bologna outside for Buddy and waiting to see if he would emerge, which he didn't, Lily headed into the den to deal with the Amazon boxes. There were hundreds of them. They were all shapes and sizes, some already broken down, but most of them stacked inside each other, on top of each other, and leaning on each other, some still full of those strange inflatable bags that cushioned the goods inside. She found the new scissors in the kitchen and went to the smallest stack of boxes to begin breaking them down into flat pieces. Some of the larger stacks were so tall that she would have to pull them down like a giant Jenga game and just get out of their way as they fell and slid all over the room. For a bunch of messy piles made by a messy person, they all seemed to be perfectly balanced. Whoever had stacked them had shown a strange amount of care for something they obviously did not care about.

She put the *Mean Girls* musical soundtrack on and developed a rhythm as she sliced the tape on each box and flattened it. She then picked up the discarded airbags and punctured them with tiny snips, deflating them as she went and tossing them into a large box, shoving them down to make more room as they collected. When she moved to one of the taller stacks, she shouted, "Take that, Regina George!" and punched the middle box, then danced back as cardboard tumbled to the ground in time with the music.

Somewhere behind all the remaining piles she heard an odd sound, so she turned off the music and listened hard. It came again, almost like a gasp, like the sound a cat made when it was surprised. It was possible that animals were living back there— possums or raccoons or rats—although it was strange that any wild thing would've stayed there once her family had moved in and started to make noise. Half-curious and half-scared, Lily kicked some of the boxes, making the huge piles shudder and dance, hoping that would be enough to send whatever it was skittering into the light.

"Get out of here," she shouted firmly from her diaphragm to make her voice loud and imposing. "Go on. Shoo."

There was a rustle again and a sort of sigh. Definitely something back there. She went to the kitchen and got the broom, holding it by the handle as she poked the bristled end into the shadowy darkness in the corner behind the boxes.

When the broom poked something that wasn't cardboard, something that very definitely felt like flesh, she jerked it back, disgusted and also terrified, her hands shaking. Whatever that thing was . . . it was bigger than anything she'd expected. Not a cat, not a possum, definitely not some harmless little mouse. And it didn't feel like it was alive.

It felt like a body.

11.

THIS TIME, LILY WASN'T GOING TO FACE WHATEVER IT WAS ALONE. IF there was something strange to see, she wanted her mom to see it, too. But she wasn't going to set the wrong tone by acting overly dramatic. She was going to be controlled. Poised. Rational.

"Mom!" she called. "I need some help, if you have a moment."

When her mom shuffled into the room, she had that now-familiar look of exhaustion and frustration, as if she were battling a mountain on her own and making little headway.

"What's up, honey?" she asked. "What is it?"

Lily handed her mom the broom. "Something back there made a noise, like an animal. So I poked it with the broom and . . . it felt like there was something there. Maybe a raccoon or something."

Her mom walked around the remaining boxes, nodding

firmly toward the work Lily had accomplished and smiling her appreciation. As she hunched over and slid the broom between the boxes and into the shadows beyond, Lily held her breath. It's like there were two sides to this house: Sometimes she saw an old, sad, unloved place that just needed a little elbow grease and hope, and other times she saw something that was twisted with rot and fungus and overgrowth, something that had gone dark to its roots and just wanted to be left alone again to crumble away to dust. Maybe whatever happened now, with her mother there as a witness, would reveal the truth of the place.

"I just feel cardboard," her mom said. "And right there, where you hear the straw scraping, that's the wall. What do you think you felt?"

Lily moved to the place where she'd crouched when she'd poked something with the broom. "Try over here," she said. "It was low on the ground."

Her mom obligingly changed places with her, and when she shoved the broom in that same spot, Lily knew the moment her mom felt it, too.

"Huh. Yeah, there it is. That's strange. Let's dig it out."

Her mom stood and began tossing down the highest boxes, letting them tumble all over the room they had so painstakingly cleaned. Lily helped, too, because she knew she was expected to, but she didn't try quite as hard as Mom did. Something about that lump, that fleshy, yielding *something,* made Lily want to hang back.

Her mom waded in deeper, tossing boxes back over her shoulder. For a moment Lily couldn't see her at all. Her mom was only five foot two, and panic raced up Lily's spine as she considered what would happen if the boxes swallowed her mom and she never came out again. It was a silly thought, on the surface, and not something she would have considered before she'd slept in this strange house and seen the things she'd seen.

But now she was beginning to see everything differently, like the way she saw the swamp outside: Perhaps it looked simple on the surface, maybe even pretty, but no one knew what lurked underneath. Dark water hid its depths, the swamp obscured its dangers, and something in this house always seemed to wait in the shadows.

Lily moved so she could see deeper into the pile of fallen boxes. They were no longer in neat stacks but had fallen in pieces like a giant child's wooden blocks knocked over during a tantrum. And somewhere back in the corner, on the floor in the shadows, she saw . . . a shape. It looked like a child curled up, their arms around their knees. And as Lily watched, two green eyes turned toward her, shining like an animal caught in a car's headlights, as the child-thing unwrapped itself and began to crawl toward her.

Lily yelped and stumbled back. She couldn't breathe, and her legs didn't want to move. She tripped on the pile of cardboard, landing inside a box and falling into it with her arms and legs flailing. Her butt hit the bottom of the box, and she struggled to stand. She could no longer see over the edge of her cardboard cage, but she could hear a horrible sound coming from the corner. It sounded like wet hands and feet crawling toward her over the boxes, sure of their path and as unstoppable as a Florida storm. A cold hand grasped her ankle, soft and clammy as a mushroom, and a rough voice whispered, "Are you ready to play with me?"

"Mom!" Lily screamed, and the hand released her foot. She could hear the cardboard shifting under someone's weight.

"Did you fall?" Her mom's warm, normal hand grasped hers and pulled her out of the box. "I'm sorry to laugh, but you look like a confused turtle."

Lily stood, but everything inside of her sank. She'd never been this scared before, like she was being hunted by some horrifying creature, and her mom was just . . . laughing at her?

"Did you see it?" Lily asked, scanning the crazy pile of boxes. She didn't see anything unusual now. The child-shaped thing was just . . . gone.

"See what?" Mom answered. Which meant no. If she'd seen what Lily had seen, felt, and heard, there would have been no question, no calm discussion.

"The thing behind the boxes," Lily pressed. "What was it?"

"Oh, that. Pretty weird. It's a beanbag chair, still in its

plastic bag. I guess they must have ordered it, and it wasn't what they wanted. Maybe they were going to return it? It looks like it's in perfect condition. Do you want it?"

Mom dragged an awkward object over and dropped it in front of Lily. It was indeed a lime-green beanbag chair. It looked like it would be comfortable for watching TV. And a part of Lily wanted it. But the louder part of her, the scared part of her, knew that if it was still in its plastic there must be something desperately wrong with it. Maybe not with the chair itself. But there must've been a reason that it hadn't been used, which made her not want to use it.

And touching it would always remind her of that soft, fleshy mushroom feeling, of the crawling child-thing that had gripped her ankle.

"No thanks. Wouldn't go with my room."

Her mom considered it. "Then maybe we should donate it. Seems like it would make some kid pretty happy."

But Lily didn't want to touch it, and she didn't think that giving it to anyone else would be any better. Not that she could explain that to her mother in any way that would make sense.

"Maybe," she said. "But it still seems kind of gross, just passing it on. There could've been bugs laying eggs in it or something." She paused before asking, "So there was nothing else back there? No sign of . . . animals?"

Her mom shook her head. "Nope. Just the beanbag. But

to be fair, when you poke it with a broom, it does feel a lot like . . . I'm not going to say an animal, but it feels like something that definitely isn't cardboard. Gave you a scare, huh?"

Lily didn't even know how to answer that question. Her mom, who'd known her every day of her life and who was trained to help people who were scared or suffering, clearly couldn't tell that she was terrified out of her mind right now. Lily wasn't being melodramatic, she wasn't trying to get attention; she was overwhelmed with panic and could barely speak. Whatever she was seeing, whatever she was experiencing . . . her mom just didn't get it. And maybe she wasn't ever going to.

Being scared like this made her feel small and uncertain. It was the opposite of drama—it took something away from her, robbed her of her confidence and control. When she was acting or being melodramatic, she knew exactly what she was doing and why. She had an audience and made herself big for them, connected with them. But this feeling—knowing she wasn't trusted, wasn't seen—made her want to shrink into a puddle.

And, of course, she knew what happened to people who saw things that weren't there. They ended up in the hospital, talking to doctors all day, trying to prove they weren't crazy. She just felt so adrift, like she couldn't tell what was true and what was imagination.

"It was just weird," she finally said. "Do you know if anything unusual ever happened here? At this house?"

Mom looked up, wary. "Unusual like what?"

"Like . . . I don't know. Someone dying here?"

Mom sighed, nudging the beanbag with her foot. "Well, it's Florida, so they don't have to tell us anything. I'm sure it's just a normal house and whoever lived here had some bad luck."

She met Lily's eyes, and Lily thought maybe her mom wasn't telling her the full truth.

"Hey, listen. There's nothing you need to worry about." Mom reached out, rubbed Lily's shoulder. "Your imagination can be such a gift, but it can also be scary. It can make a story out of anything, can't it?"

Lily wasn't sure if that was a compliment or an insult, but she could tell she wasn't going to get any more info out of her mom on the topic. "I guess. But, um, would you mind taking the beanbag thing out to the dumpster while I keep on with the boxes here?"

Her mom gave her that understanding kind of mom smile, the kind that said that Lily wasn't making sense, but she was just a kid, so that was okay.

"Sure, honey. You're doing a good job. I couldn't do it without your help—all this cleanup. It felt pretty hopeless at first, but now it's actually coming together. I think we're going to be really happy here, once our stuff shows up, and we do a little DIY."

"Hope so," Lily said. Even though she'd practiced her smile

in the mirror millions of times, it felt unnatural and strange just now.

Her mom hefted the beanbag awkwardly and dragged it toward the door. She had to contort it to get it through, and Lily shivered as she realized it looked like the beanbag was fighting her mother, trying to wriggle back in through the door.

12.

LILY FELT IMMEDIATELY BETTER THE MOMENT THE BEANBAG CHAIR
was out of the house. She remembered Mrs. Burrell explaining
fight or flight in biology last year and assuring the class that
any kind of busy activity would help dispel that shaky feeling,
so the moment her mom was back inside, she returned to the
pile of cardboard. With quivering hands, she began viciously
breaking down the boxes, trying not to think too hard about
the cold, dead fingers that had grasped her foot, and the raspy,
ravaged voice that had spoken to her, as intimate as a whisper
in her ear. Even if she had imagined it, it was not a pleasant
thing to imagine. Why couldn't her brain imagine fun things,
like unicorns and cupcakes and randomly meeting the cast of
Hamilton in a Starbucks in Times Square?

*I'm okay. I'm okay. Everything is okay. It's my imagination.
It's the stuffy air.*

She refocused on the boxes. There *was* something soothing about physical labor. Each box had to be sliced where it was taped together, popped apart until it was flat, and then settled onto a stack with the bigger boxes on the bottom. When a stack got big enough, she carried the heavy cardboard flats outside two at a time and tossed them in the dumpster, where they settled as neatly as slices of bread. It should've been easy work, but she couldn't stop thinking about what it felt like, poking something with the broom and imagining that it was a dead body. She couldn't stop reliving the moment when it seemed something had crawled at her, and she'd remained stuck in that box, helpless, and the cold fingers touched her leg, over and over in her mind—and then the scissors slipped and she sliced her middle finger wide open.

This time when she called her mom, she didn't try to sound calm or reasonable. She'd cut deep, and the blood was welling out, dripping on the pile of dusty brown cardboard. Her mom was by her side in a heartbeat, kneeling, worried. She didn't have to ask what was wrong. She could see it. Even through her panic, Lily was flooded with relief that finally, finally someone was taking her seriously.

"Okay, honey. It's going to be okay. Let me go see if I can find some Band-Aids," her mom said calmly, stroking the sweaty hair away from Lily's forehead.

"But . . . so much blood . . ." Lily felt it happen—the swoon.

She hated seeing her own blood. Her mom caught her as she fell, and Lily was kind of there and kind of not. Shadows danced in her vision, everything washed over red with sparkling pinpricks like fireworks.

"Whoa, there, honey," her mom said gently, helping her sit up. "It's not as bad as all that."

"Easy to say when you're not the one bleeding," Lily murmured weakly. "I've lost a gallon of blood already."

Her mom chuckled. "That's how I know you're going to be all right. You're being snarky and melodramatic. Now, just stay here for a minute. Hold it for me. You're going to be fine, I promise." Mom wrapped Lily's good hand around the cut and held it firmly to show her what to do. Lily tried to ignore the slippery feel of her own blood and the bright smell of salt and copper overlaying the house's constant scent of dust and rot. She struggled to keep her eyes open. If she closed them again . . . that thing might come back and touch her.

She felt the exact moment her mom left the room. It was as if the sun stopped shining. And, well, it had. The sky was gray now, and it looked like it was going to rain. That was one thing her mother had told her about Florida: You could have a perfectly bright sunny day, and then suddenly a crazy thunderstorm would show up out of nowhere and rage for twenty minutes, then go away, and it would be a bright day again.

"Here we are," her mom said. She was holding an ancient

box of Band-Aids. Seriously ancient. They didn't have car-
toon characters on them, and they weren't in a variety of skin
colors. They were just plain, peach-colored, rubber-smelling
Band-Aids.

"How old are these?" Lily asked with a sad little laugh.
"Do they even work still? Am I going to get some weird old
disease?"

But her mom, the registered nurse, was already busy taking
care of things. Since they didn't have the usual first aid supplies, she had Lily wash the cut well with soap and water in
the sink and dry it off with paper towels. Then she laboriously
unwrapped one of the old Band-Aids and stuck it around Lily's
finger. It was too tight and felt kind of gross, but at least she
wasn't bleeding anymore.

"See? No big deal. Good as new."

Lily was trying to think of a reason to keep her mom there
so she wouldn't be alone, and thankfully her mom sensed her
unease. "You just flatten the boxes," Mom told her. "I'll handle
the scissors. We'll finish it together and then it will be done,
and then lunch. How about that?"

It went faster that way. Mom sliced the boxes, Lily flattened
them, and they worked together to carry them out and stack
them in the dumpster before the rain began. Lily noted that the
bean bag chair wasn't in the dumpster—it was in the back of
Mom's car. She didn't mention it, though. All the fight had

gone out of her. Soon, wonder of wonders, the room was completely empty of cardboard. And it was transformed.

When Lily had first seen it, it had seemed like a rotting nightmare labyrinth of looming garbage and sinister shadows. Now it was just a den like any other, if a little droopy and outdated. The couch and love seat were arranged around an entertainment center that had once held dusty VHS cassettes and some old science-fiction novels. Mom had gotten rid of those early on. They just felt so personal. Same with the old leather recliner that smelled like BO and matched the destroyed one outside. Lily was glad to see them both gone—there was something sad about the matched pair. She was curious why only one of them had been dragged outside originally, though. There were now two bright spots of wood where they'd once sat.

When the family's storage container arrived, they would finally have all the pieces they needed to make the space feel like home. They had better couches. They had a nicer entertainment center. They had rugs to cover those odd bright spots. They had their bookshelves and books and pictures, and soon this room would not look bare and sad. It would be a place where they could make their own memories.

Now it just felt empty. But empty was better than haunted.

Empty was better than riddled with hiding places for . . . whatever that had been.

They took a break for lunch right as the storm hit. Mom

offered to go out for fast food and ice cream, but then black clouds rolled in and rain fell like a hammer, making home seem like a much drier option. The house went dark as the storm raged, so they turned on all the lights and cooked grilled cheese sandwiches in a shiny new pan. They had potato chips and apples and snack cakes. Since they had to live in the unfinished house, Mom had loosened up about junk food.

When they were done, and Lily had made sure there was nothing else she could help with, she went to her bathroom to make sure she didn't look like she'd been spelunking in a cave of dust bunnies. She didn't have expensive clothes like Rachel, but she wanted to look her best, so she brushed her long, dark hair into a ponytail and changed into clean shorts free of swamp mud and bloodstains.

Just as her mom had promised, the storm battered the house like crazy and then quit suddenly, leaving the world a magical golden green that glittered with raindrops. Lily grabbed some lunch meat on her way out and went to hang around near the dock. Her phone was now fully charged and had three bars. She had a little time before Rachel's arrival that she planned to fill by texting CJ some *Newsies* GIFs. Maybe Buddy would even show up again and she could convince him to succumb to belly rubs using tidbits of ham.

The old wood of the dock was dark and slick with rain. The water itself was cloudy black, even harder to see through than yesterday since it had been stirred up by the storm. She didn't want to sit down on the wet, spongy boards, so she stood around hopping from foot to foot. There was no sign of Buddy, but then again, he seemed to want to remain hidden. Only the promise of food had brought him out before.

"Hey, Buddy. Here, boy," she called, tearing off a piece of ham and waggling it in the air, hoping he would smell it or see it and come running.

For a few minutes, nothing happened, and she took a few pics of the creepy swamp and sent them to CJ. But then she heard a rustling in the woods. If she hadn't seen Buddy before, if she hadn't been a hundred percent certain that he was just a poor lost dog, she might have been afraid that something worse was coming through the forest toward her. But she could hear it now, the sound of his tail wagging at the certainty of supper. The dog appeared, trembling, looking like the storm had battered him. His thickly matted hair was wetted down and heavy, making him a dark, dirty gray, like some hideous swamp monster. His black eyes flashed through the bedraggled tendrils, desperate. She tossed him a piece of meat.

The poor dog gobbled it up without even tasting it. When he looked at her again, she saw a sort of devotion shining in his eyes. She tossed him another piece of meat, and he devoured it.

"How would you feel about some grooming, huh? Maybe a bath? You need to get shaved down. I could bring out some scissors at least. So you could see better."

His tail thumped uncertainly. Maybe he recognized one of those words and didn't like it. Lily didn't know much about dogs or their care, but she knew that this dog had been loved once and now missed it. And he desperately needed attention. She tossed down her last piece of meat and said, "Stay here, Buddy. I'll bring you more food."

She ran inside and grabbed some more meat before her mom could see it. She also snatched the crusts from her grilled cheese from the top of the trash can. Then she picked up the scissors, being careful to hold the points clutched in her fist while she jogged outside. She was painfully aware that now was not a good time to forget scissor safety.

Buddy was waiting for her. He must've understood that more food would be coming, or at least he had high hopes. She tossed down the crusts and patted his head. This time he didn't flinch. After some comforting scratches and pats, she grabbed up a wad of the long matted hair on his forehead and snipped it off with her scissors. Buddy jerked away in surprise, but then he looked at her with eyes that were actually a warm chocolate-cake brown, and she could almost see him telling her thank you. As she fed him bits of meat, she used her scissors to snip off the bigger clumps of fur and freed his tail so that it could fully wag again. She snipped around his legs, where old mats made it hard for him to move. He didn't seem to like the process, but he didn't hate it. Maybe he was ready to trust again.

Buddy heard Rachel's boat right before Lily did. He bolted into the forest and wouldn't return no matter how many times she called him. Rachel deftly parked at the dock and waved.

"Kyle said you wouldn't be here," she said. "But I thought you might. Was that your dog?"

Before stepping onto the boat, Lily rubbed her hands on her shorts, hoping that she didn't smell like lunch meat and old, dirty dog.

"Not mine. But he used to live here, I think. He had a collar on when I saw him the first time, and the tags had this address. His name is Buddy. Have you seen him before?" She sat on the boat seat, but Rachel kept looking at the house, too curious to pull away from the dock.

Rachel's brow drew down. "I think I've seen him? He used to look a lot better, though. He would get loose and go for runs. I saw a little kid on the main road once, hollering and squeaking a toy. A girl. She had short hair. But when I called out to her, she ran away."

Rachel paused. It looked like something was bothering her, or maybe she wasn't sure what to say. And Rachel didn't seem like someone who was often at a loss for words.

"I don't know if it was this house," she said. "But I remember something happening around here, on this side of the lake. Couple of years ago. We saw the lights through the trees. Fire trucks and ambulances. Lots of police, red and blue flashing, you know? Everybody on the bus was talking about it. And then Kyle said there was caution tape on the dock for a while. I never really thought about it, but . . . I think maybe something really bad happened here."

Rachel's eyes went wide. "Somebody said the little girl died."

13.

LILY'S HEART FLUTTERED FOR A MOMENT, BUT THEN SHE CONNECTED the dots.

"I bet it was the old man. I heard my parents say it was *natural,* and I found some old prescriptions he didn't fill, so I think he actually died here. That's why the house is so gross. The little girl probably went to live somewhere else after that."

"I don't know," Rachel said, staring toward the house, shielding her eyes with a hand. "There's this urban legend about a little ghost girl running down the middle of the street at night. Kyle said he saw her once when some junior was driving him home in the rain. He said the ghost looked like she was confused, looking for something."

"Do you know what her name was?"

"The girl who lived here, or the ghost girl? Neither. This kid at my school named Jaiden said she was murdered, but he lies all the time."

"Where do you go to school?" Lily asked her, switching subjects before Rachel thought she was weird for asking too many questions about ghosts.

Of course, she couldn't stop thinking about a murdered ghost girl running barefoot down the long, dark road, but her next biggest worry was definitely school. Mom hadn't yet mentioned which school she would be attending, but she knew there were several choices in the area.

"Amblewood Prep. It's off the highway, a couple of miles down. It's a private school. I kind of hate it, but I think I would kind of hate any school. Do you know where you're going?"

"Not yet. We've only been here a couple of days. We don't even have Wi-Fi yet."

Rachel shrugged and steered the boat into the lake. "Oh well. We've got two months until school, so who cares? Now I'll show you the cool parts of Lake Silence."

They were out all afternoon. Rachel had brought supplies: sunblock, bug repellent, fishing poles, bread, binoculars, a birding book, and, most important, snacks. Lily was glad to learn that even though Rachel looked like one of the popular girls from back home, she was nice and not catty at all. She was kind of a nerd, too. She had a list of birds in the back of her book and she got really excited when she got to check off a new one she hadn't seen before. Her enthusiasm actually made Lily kind of care about birds for a little while. And when Lily told her there was a musical for *Tuck Everlasting,* which was one of Rachel's favorite books, Rachel promised she'd listen to the soundtrack. Then Lily caught her first fish, a bluegill, and she was glad that Rachel didn't mind removing the hook so they could throw it back. But Lily absolutely refused to kiss the fish on the lips, a weird custom that Rachel said meant she would catch the fish again. Lily did not want to catch another fish badly enough to kiss this one. There were, apparently, limits to her drama, and kissing fish was one of them.

The sun was just starting to set when Rachel pulled the boat back up to Lily's dock. Lily had told her that she needed to be home before dinner, not only so her parents wouldn't be annoyed with her again, but also because it just got creepy out here after dark . . . especially after hearing about the caution tape and the ghost girl.

"Thanks for the tour," she said as she stepped onto the wobbling dock.

"No worries," Rachel said with a smile. "It's cool to have someone nearby to hang with. Our neighborhood is mostly rich old people, and they kind of hate seeing anyone under sixty having fun. If you want to come over tomorrow, we can jump on the trampoline and swim and play video games or whatever. Kyle won't be there, so we'll have the house to ourselves."

"Your parents let you stay home alone all day?" Lily asked.

Rachel rolled her eyes. "No. Carla is always there, even though we basically ignore her. She's been around since Kyle was a baby."

Lily hadn't been alone that much in her life, either. Her mom had always arranged her schedule so that she could be home in the afternoon, and her parents didn't go out on dates very often. She needed to ask her mom when she would start her new job at the hospital and what her hours would be like here. She hadn't considered the possibility yet, but she didn't really want to be alone in the new house, especially after dark.

She thanked Rachel again, and the boat pulled away, leaving a shimmering wake in the colors of the sunset. Back home in Colorado, Lily mostly stuck with CJ and the drama kids en masse, and her social calendar was always busy around the fall musical and spring play. She'd never really hung out with just one person who lived nearby. Of course, Lily knew she wouldn't be going to the expensive private school that Rachel attended—the only reason they were here was that they were super broke—but it would be nice to know she had someone within walking distance to hang with on the weekends. And hopefully for the rest of the summer.

She quickly got off the rickety old dock—it just never felt safe. The green weeds of the yard still sparkled with raindrops. She could see the path Buddy had taken when he hurriedly escaped into the forest, because he'd left a dark trail through the droplets. The afternoon was edging into dusk, but there was still a blazing orange light limning every edge as the brilliant sun sank behind the stark black trees, a legacy of the storm. Lily had not yet gone into that part of the forest, over on the right side of her house, so she took a few steps in that direction, following Buddy's path and wondering where he spent all his time.

It was an odd sort of forest, very different from the tall old trees in Colorado with the mountains always standing vigilant behind them. This patch of woods seemed very sharp by comparison, with low spiky plants that looked like something dinosaurs would eat, shaped like giant pineapples or cacti without the spines. The plants grew tightly together and were difficult to get past. As she tried to push in deeper, the leaves plucked at her shirt and scratched her legs. Overhead, the larger trees were hung with gray moss that cast shimmering, shivering shade on the silvery ground down below. Those strange, striped shadows seemed to move in a breeze that never quite reached Lily's skin.

"Here, Buddy," she called, but she didn't hear him hurrying through the brush. The sky was getting rust-colored now, like the blood she'd dripped on the cardboard earlier. The shadows darkened, and suddenly Lily remembered the snake in the swamp. There were more snakes like that everywhere, and her sneakers wouldn't save her from venom-filled fangs.

She began to back out of the forest, but the branches scratched her spine and slithered over her shoulders, seeming to clutch her close. She spun around, and she couldn't even see her house through the thickly clustered greenery. It felt eerily similar to when she'd gotten lost in the swamp, only now, instead of thick, sucking wet, she felt the dry, scratching, snarling thorns of the forest closing in around her.

Suddenly, she felt like a trapped animal. Like she was being purposefully blocked. She reached down for her phone and felt the long spines of a plant scrape across the skin of her arm, leaving a raised red mark. Something tickled her ankle, and when she looked down, she saw a vine curling around her foot. She yanked it away, and it stung her hand with prickers.

A noise deeper in the forest made her freeze.

It didn't sound like Buddy, tentative and shivering and shy.

It sounded thick and slow and stupid, cracking branches and shuffling through leaves.

Panic took hold of her heart, and she ripped and tore at the twigs and vines reaching for her, stumbling backward, tripping, falling, turning, clawing away.

"Just let me go," she pled. "Please, just let me go!"

Lily pushed with both arms, ferocious and fierce and unafraid of the scratches, and the branches blocking her suddenly gave way. She stumbled into her own yard. The car was gone. Her mom must have gone to pick up her dad—much later than usual. Lily took a step toward the house and stopped. She had never felt this alone. Was it worse to be outside in the dark, or inside that strange old house where she couldn't always trust her own eyes—and where she knew roaches and spiders lurked, whether or not the ones she had seen were real? What would it feel like to turn the doorknob and find it locked?

At least her mother had left the outside light on. The bulb beside the door cast a warm glow, and as soon as Lily stepped into its shine, she felt a little better.

Looking out at the lake from here, she could see the fading brilliance of the dregs of sunset reflected in the flat black water. She couldn't see the houses across the lake, thanks to a rise of cattails and water plants. But it gave her some comfort to know that they were there. And that Rachel and Kyle were nearby, looking out at the same lake and seeing something they knew, something fun to explore. She considered what her dock might have looked like covered in yellow caution tape. But the wood was so wobbly and old and rotten, she could only envision the tape in a similarly sad state, breaking away by itself, fading from a bright yellow to the color of an old man's teeth.

She looked down at her phone. No bars. When they had Wi-Fi again and the family computer arrived, she was going to find out exactly what had happened at this house. Surely her mom had Googled their address before they bought it, to make sure nothing horrible had happened? Sure, it was Florida, but shouldn't people have to tell you if a house had . . . if someone had . . . if someone had died inside a house, before they sold it to you? An old man dying naturally was one thing, but a little girl? A murder?

That was a lot scarier, and definitely not natural.

Lily heard a rumble coming toward her, and when she looked toward the long driveway, bright lights blinded her. She threw up her arm to shield herself as the car honked cheerfully. Like anyone could be cheerful here, now.

The car rolled to a stop. Mom and Dad got out, and Mom was carrying take-out bags. Lily could smell Chinese food, and her stomach growled. Rachel's packaged snacks were great, but hot food was so much better.

"I left the door unlocked," Mom called. "Is it stuck? We need to get you a key."

Lily realized something, and asked her mom, "Don't we need to have the locks changed? I mean, whoever used to live here . . . they don't seem like they were . . ." She wanted to say *sane* but recognized that it wasn't a kind thing to say. She was really just trying to ask if there was a chance Britney was still living nearby. "I just mean, what if they came back?"

"We already told you no one's coming back, sweetie," her dad said with that fake cheerfulness that insulted Lily's feelings as a kid and an actor. "We don't need to change the locks. We'll make some extra keys tomorrow. The realtor only gave us the one set, and it's pretty old and beat up."

Mom opened the door, which did stick a little, and Lily followed the Chinese food inside. Her dad came in last, and he turned off the outside light and locked the door behind them. He'd been out of work for so long that seeing him in a suit, looking so focused and determined, made him seem like a stranger. Of course, he had felt like a stranger at home in his pajamas in Colorado, too, as he looked for jobs and grew a beard and their grocery budget dwindled and Lily's requests for new boots got denied and she caught him frowning and kind of staring through her when he thought she wasn't looking. He didn't even seem to know that he was doing it.

And Mom had picked up so many extra shifts that she'd started to lose weight and catch every cold, and then she missed the spring musical and didn't get to see Lily star as Ariel in *The Little Mermaid,* and . . . well, that was one good thing about Florida. The family would supposedly get back to normal, whatever that was.

Dad went to change clothes and Mom opened up the square white boxes of food. The room smelled so good that Lily almost drooled a little. She dished out her favorite, sweet and sour chicken and spring rolls, plus plenty of fluffy white rice. Their family had never been particularly formal, so Lily just grabbed her chopsticks and dug in.

"How was work?" Lily asked her dad, following his script.

"Good," he answered, looking up like he was surprised that she had spoken. "Mom said you were really helpful today. That's good—we see you toeing the line. I know the move has been hard on you and it's no fun being stuck in the house, but I think things are going to get better."

He asked her about her day, and she skipped the part with

the boxes and told him about fishing with Rachel and catching her first bluegill. Mom complimented her on how much work she'd gotten done, and for a moment there, Lily basked in her own little spotlight. They saw her. They were smiling at her. No drama necessary. No one mentioned anything bad that she'd done, now or in the past. No one mentioned Colorado. For now, they just *were*.

It was a pretty good night.

After dinner, Lily skipped upstairs to her room before she remembered that something might be amiss. It was odd, how she thought of it now as *her* room in *their* house, but she still didn't feel comfortable being in the house or being in her room. Every time she came back, she knew there was a possibility that she'd find something new and strange and terrible, or that she might find her bed torn apart yet again and those harsh words scrawled in ash-gray letters.

But nothing was wrong this time. Everything was as she'd left it. And when she tried her phone—which her mom had forgotten to reclaim—she had those same three bars. She spent the rest of the night texting with CJ, telling him about how gross the house had been and how much fun she had on the boat—but not about the horrible things that had happened to her, the impossible things she had seen. She didn't want him to think she was going crazy. Drama was one thing, but it had to be believable. The actor's job was to make the audience *believe.* And the things that were happening? It just wasn't believable. So she left that part out.

Instead, she told him how the house looked like it was half buried in the swamp by a giant. She told him about the strange dog that she was trying to tame, and the odd Jurassic Park beauty of the forest, and the depth of the lake and how the sunset reflected on it like fire. She told him about the funny young birds that looked like dinosaurs and the ancient turtles that looked like mossy logs and sometimes dragged themselves up out of the water and blinked their black eyes like they'd forgotten their glasses. She told him how the air felt as heavy as pound cake, and how her hair had developed a frizzy curl that it never had in Colorado.

But she didn't tell him any of the scary things. She didn't tell anyone.

She was beginning to think maybe she'd imagined all of it.

Until she woke up in the early morning and realized she wasn't alone.

14.

THE ROOM WAS ALMOST PITCH DARK WHEN LILY OPENED HER EYES. She'd had trouble going to sleep and had just awakened from a nightmare—she knew that much. She couldn't remember the specifics, only that she had felt trapped somewhere in the dark, and that she couldn't breathe. She sat up. Her thrashing had flung her sheet and comforter to the floor. The only light came from the moon, shining around the edges of her blinds.

The house had air-conditioning, but it didn't quite seem to reach her room upstairs. It was always warm up here. It reminded her of a sponge that had been wrung out but still felt damp when you touched it. And her fan wouldn't turn on all the way. Well, it would, but then the lightbulbs rattled in their cups, and she worried that the whole thing would fall on the foot of her bed and chop off her legs, even if that seemed a bit far-fetched. So it made sense that she was covered in sweat, her hair plastered to her forehead and neck.

"He runs away sometimes. His address is on the tags. They'll bring him home."

That's why the sound was so familiar—it was Buddy's collar. And someone was playing with it. Someone who should not be here. And wasn't that collar in a drawer downstairs?

But Lily couldn't speak. Whenever she tried to scream in her nightmares, her throat would go dry—and now, when she most wanted to call out to her parents, her voice stubbornly wouldn't work. For a moment she questioned it: Was she asleep? Was this one of those dreams where she was paralyzed, and things seemed real but weren't? She remembered a trick she had learned to tell if it was a dream or not—you just had to look at something with numbers on it, then look away and look back. In dreams, the numbers would change, or the alarm clock would disappear. Dreams couldn't hold on to numbers. But there was nothing in her room with numbers.

Her tongue unstuck from the roof of her mouth, and she whispered, "Am I dreaming?"

The only answer was the annoyed jingling of metal and a dull scratch.

"It's not a dream," the other voice said, but it didn't sound so sure.

Instead of another metallic jingle, there was a clattering thump, like the collar had been dropped onto the floorboards. Lily heard the scratching again; it grated on her nerves, harsh as nails on a chalkboard. The shadow in the corner—was something twitching there now, something more than just a shadow? Lily couldn't move, but her eyes were still able to roll in their sockets, even as tears pricked their corners and began to creep down her cheeks like ice.

Whatever was behind the door was moving. And it was heading toward her.

The shadow detached from the door and rose up. Fingers appeared, all white with black at the tips, flowing through the air. Lily saw hair, dark, ragged hair, rising up as if floating. It reminded her of the Van de Graaff machine she'd seen once at a museum, the way it made her hair float as the electricity coursed harmlessly through her.

But there was nothing harmless about this . . . thing.

The shadow swirled and its shape changed and blurred, sometimes just a shadow and sometimes a child. Its eyes were dark holes, black as ink, black as lake water stirred up by the thunderstorm. The thing didn't whisper again, but it seemed to quiver and shake like TV static. An unearthly sound filled the room, like a mixture of wind and screaming that was muffled by thick glass.

Lily knew she was frozen, but just like in a dream, she had to try to make a sound. So she willed her mouth to move and she screamed and screamed and screamed and screamed. It seemed to go on forever, the black shadow growing and reaching for her with fingers like fern fronds slick with rain. All Lily could feel was terror and the ice-cold prickling of her own fingers and toes. She couldn't unwrap her hands from around her knees, her body seeking to roll itself into the tiniest ball possible, to be the smallest target.

"I want to show you," the voice whispered.

And then suddenly her mother was there, pushing the door open the rest of the way with a meaty *thunk* and flicking on the light.

"Lily, are you okay? I heard screaming."

Lily's fingers unlatched from her knees, but she didn't dare put her feet on the ground. She scooted her back against the brass bed frame and scanned the room, checking every single corner revealed by the overhead light for any remaining spots of unnatural shadow.

"I . . . ," she started. Of all the things that had just occurred, all the things that didn't seem quite real, it was strange to think that her screaming actually *was* real. Because that was the part that felt the most like a dream.

"I had a nightmare," she finally said.

Her mom looked blurry and exhausted, with marks like purple thumbprints under her eyes, but she smiled and pattered across the wooden floorboards to sit beside Lily and wrap her in a hug. Funny that this, finally, was the traumatic event worthy of comfort.

"Nightmares are the worst," her mom said. "I've been having them, too."

"You have?" Lily asked. "What are yours about?"

Her mom chuckled that sad adult chuckle that said Lily wouldn't understand grown-up fears until she was having them herself. "They're just typical stress dreams. Anxiety stuff. My teeth are falling out, or growing long roots like vines, or crumbling in my mouth like crackers. I had one where your dad turned into a werewolf. Dreams can be so weird. But they don't always mean something. I find that comforting. What was your nightmare about?"

"This house," Lily said, her voice very low, almost as if she didn't want the house to hear. "It's just so different here. It's like this place has secrets. In the forest and the lake and the swamp . . . It's just . . ."

"A different world," her mom finished for her. "For all of us. And we didn't have much choice about coming here, so that makes it harder."

"We're the ones doing all the work, it feels like," Lily said angrily. Something about the fact that they were the only ones awake made it feel okay to say something so brazen against her father.

"It's hard on Dad, too," her mom said softly. "What happened back home . . . He took it hard. But he's so determined I think he talked himself into believing that this place would be nicer. Easier."

"It's not nice or easy."

"Believe me, I know. But hey, it's getting better. We're making good headway. And our storage container should arrive next week. You'll feel different once we have everything from home. What we're doing now . . . it almost feels like the Oregon Trail, doesn't it? Traveling somewhere new and strange and not having all the things you need to be happy and feel safe there?"

Lily just nodded. She thought, but did not say, that the defining trait of the video game *Oregon Trail* was that pretty much everyone died.

"You okay now?" Mom asked. "Nightmare banished?"

Lily licked her lips. Sure, she was twelve, but that was still young enough to be scared by nightmares, wasn't it? "Would you mind checking behind the door? That's where . . . There was . . ."

"A monster?" Mom gave her a fond smile. "Someone's been reading scary books again."

"Uh, yeah. You caught me," Lily said, because that was easier than the truth.

Mom hugged her, kissed her on the forehead with warm, dry lips, and stood up.

"I think we need an escape today," she said, running fingers through Lily's hair. "Maybe ice cream or a movie?" She looked up and frowned. "Somewhere with lots of AC."

The tiniest fraction of Lily's heart warmed. "That would be good."

Mom walked to the door and pulled it away from the wall. Lily's heart was thumping like crazy, and it didn't slow down when the shadows revealed a strange glimmer on the ground.

"What's this?" Mom asked. She leaned down and picked something up, making an all-too-familiar jingling sound.

When she held up Buddy's dirty old collar, every hair on Lily's body stood up on end.

15.

LILY JUST SAT THERE WITH HER MOUTH HANGING OPEN, BUT THEN HER mom shook her head. "Wait, why do you have this filthy old collar? I put it away. Have you been playing with that dog I told you not to touch?"

In no mood to argue over it, Lily said, "Can we talk about this in the morning? Please?"

She must have looked as exhausted and freaked out as she felt, because her mother stopped staring at her sternly, her face softened, and she came back over to stroke Lily's hair. "I only want what's best for you. You know that. Wild dogs can have rabies and all sorts of other diseases."

Lily stared into the corner behind the door and said, "They can, but he doesn't. His name is Buddy. He used to live here, and I want to help him. He's nice, just scared."

Her mother walked back toward the door with a weary

sigh. "We'll talk about it in the morning, then. Good night, sweetheart. Sleep sweet."

"Good night, Mom," Lily said. But Mom was already heading downstairs, taking Buddy's collar with her.

Lily didn't even try to sleep after that. If she closed her eyes, the shadow might come back. It might creep out of its corner and toward her. It might reach out with cold white hands and . . . Ugh. Even the thought of the collar jangling made her blood run cold. But her mother had taken it downstairs. If it showed up again tonight . . .

Well, then she would know something was really, really, definitely wrong.

She left the light on and picked up a book to read. It was an older fantasy book, one she'd heard of before. She'd even seen the movie, she thought. She looked at the name written in the front of the book, traced it with finger. Britney West. If only she could find out what had happened to Britney. Because she didn't like what she was starting to consider.

Had she . . . just met Britney?

She didn't go downstairs right when the sun came up, even though she was awake. She let Dad get up, listened to him showering and clanking around the kitchen as he made his coffee. It smelled good and warm and real, the scent floating up the stairs, so unlike last night's strange cold moment in the dark. Her room was hot again, not that she liked it that way. The peculiar chill had fled with the shadows.

Mom and Dad both left, and then Mom came back with the car as usual. Lily could hear her going inside and outside, doors opening and closing, things being dragged this way and that. She realized she hadn't even been inside her parents' bedroom yet. How weird, to think that there were rooms in her own house she had not yet discovered. It would have been exciting if it wasn't so creepy.

The house . . . Well, it kept its own secrets.

When she finally came downstairs, her mom didn't mention what had happened last night, not the nightmare and not the dirty collar. She gave Lily her usual good-morning hug and went back to work. In between bites of cereal, Lily quietly looked around for the dog collar, but it wasn't in any of the kitchen drawers or cabinets. They were all mostly bare and empty while they waited for her family's stuff, so it would've been hard to miss.

Maybe it was in the room with her mom. Maybe there were more clues about what had happened in this house in the master bedroom. It probably had once belonged to the old man whose clothing and prescriptions she'd found in the laundry room.

Lily rinsed out her cereal bowl and went through the door into the den, which was now completely clean and mostly empty, and yet still felt somehow alien. There was a short

hallway that led to a small spare bedroom, which was still totally full of garbage—or maybe just junk, since it looked more
like what you would see at a garage sale than actual trash. After
Lily and her mom had cleaned it out, Dad would probably
claim that room as his office, even though he would just use it
for weekend napping. Considering that her closet upstairs was
tiny, Lily would've loved a room like that, to rig up curtains
and a stage and use it for practice and make a cozy reading
nook. It would've been nice to have a little space just for herself
that didn't feel like . . . well, like a ghost had already claimed it.

The hall dead-ended into the master bedroom, which had
thick shag carpet that might have felt soft and luxurious the
day it was installed but just felt old and dirty to Lily, as if de-
cades' worth of bug legs were tangled in it. She didn't like the
feeling of it touching her bare skin at all. She couldn't believe
her parents slept in there. Lily vastly preferred the plain wood
floorboards upstairs.

There was a big queen bed, but it didn't look comfortable or welcoming. It was a brass bed, the metal ancient and
tarnished. Mom and Dad's quilt looked especially ratty on it.
There was also a beat-up dresser and an old trunk, but there
were no personal decorations. No family photographs that an
old man might keep around, no books or wallets that would tell
stories about the people who'd lived here before. Her mother
had clearly given this room the same effort she had given the
others—it was empty of anyone else's memories and as clean as

she could get it. Any clues about the previous occupants were in the bottom of the dumpster.

She heard her mother muttering in the room beyond. Lily walked past two different closets to find her mom on her hands and knees, scrubbing the blackened tile of an old shower.

"So I guess now is the time to tell you that I've been using your shower and your shampoo," Mom said, trying to joke around despite the fact that Lily could tell she was upset. "My shower looks like it was last used by the Creature from the Black Lagoon."

"Well, at least it wasn't the Wolfman," Lily said. "Can you imagine the hairballs?" Emboldened by the daylight and feeling more like her old self, she curled her hands into claws and performed a growly little pantomime about the Wolfman showering, including putting on a shower cap and trying to shave.

Her mom laughed, but she didn't stop scrubbing. At this rate they were going to go bankrupt just buying enough yellow gloves to keep this house from being swallowed by dirt.

"I've got the Wolfman bathroom covered, but can I count on you to do some more cleaning? Now that the den's better, we can branch out. And then maybe ice cream?"

Lily's heart bobbed and sank. Ice cream was great, but it didn't quite cancel out more work. She knew she had to help clean, that her mom shouldn't have to do it all herself, but she would've loved to have had some free time, or maybe something bigger to look forward to, like going to the movies or to a water park. Anything but more housework.

"I can clean, if it's not too gross," she said. Then, quickly and feeling a little guilty about it, she added, "No toilets."

"I think I have just the job for you. Have you noticed the tiny door?"

That was a line Lily had waited her entire life to hear, right up there with *Would you like the armoire that goes to Narnia?* or *Drink this adorable potion and follow that white rabbit.*

"There's a tiny door?" she asked.

Mom smiled. "Yep. I'm pretty sure it's the space under the stairs. No promises about magical worlds, but I doubt you could fit many Amazon boxes under there. Still, wear gloves and take the broom. If it's like everything else in this house . . ."

"It's going to be gross," Lily finished for her. "Probably full of millipedes."

After everything she'd seen this week, still Lily couldn't help being a little bit excited about the prospect of being the first person to see what was under the stairs. The only stairs in the house were the ones that went to her room, and she had been up and down them a hundred times without ever considering what might be in the space beneath them. It was probably just going to be more nasty hoarder garbage, but still. Garbage could be thrown away. Walls could be painted. Maybe it would be cool. Maybe she could build that reading nook she longed for that no one else could fit in and curl up in a pile of pillows to listen to musicals and text with CJ.

She went to the kitchen for gloves, paper towels, and, yes, the broom. No way would she stick her head in a dark place without giving it a good broom poking first.

She walked back to the staircase and checked all the walls around it, but she didn't see a door anywhere. Behind the staircase was the spare bedroom. On the side of the staircase was a flat wall. Which meant that the tiny door her mom was talking about had to be . . . on the outside of the house.

Her interest in the whole venture did a swan dive into the orchestra pit. If there was one thing she was learning about Florida, it was that anything outside was going to get destroyed—or at least grossified—by the elements. She could not forget that although she finally had a pool, it looked like a vat of acid slime that had swallowed a dead whale. Her mom had totally tricked her.

Taking her supplies, Lily went outside and around to the back side of the house. Oh, yes. There it was, hidden behind some overgrown plants with stabby leaves—a small door, just stuck on the side of the house, adding to the building's odd, topsy-turvy nature. The door had a keyhole and a clear glass knob, and when she turned it, it appeared to be locked. Fabulous. Now all she had to do was find a tiny key somewhere, and hopefully it wasn't already in the bottom of the dumpster with everything else they'd swept up from the filthy floor. She even crouched down to try to look under the door, but it was pitch-black inside, and she couldn't see anything.

When she reported this finding to her mother, her mother just looked around her hopeless bathroom and shrugged. "Oh well. Another mystery. Narnia will have to wait. Go . . . be a kid or something."

Lily tried not to grin too hard and walked out of the room. It occurred to her that this summer she hadn't really felt like a kid at all. They'd sprung this move on her, and she'd had only two weeks to get used to the idea and help pack up the house before they were in the car and on their way here. And since they'd been here, her world had mostly been cleaning and freaking out. Except . . .

Except for Rachel.

She went upstairs and got her phone—feeling only a little guilty that she hadn't returned it to her mom—and sent Rachel a text to see if she wanted to hang out. Rachel texted back immediately, asking if she could come check out the new house. Lily panicked for a few minutes before deciding on honesty and telling Rachel that the house was a gross mess, and none of their stuff was here yet, so it was basically like a really nasty old hotel with no place to sit. But Rachel was apparently too curious to care.

Lily asked her mom if Rachel could come over, and Mom was more than glad to meet the first friend she'd made in the area. She even offered to order out lunch for them, although

Lily was sure that sandwiches would be fine. She ran to her bathroom, brushed out her hair, and made sure she looked okay before she went to the dock to wait. The boat turned up shortly after that, and Rachel was bubbling with excitement.

"Oh my gosh, this place is so mysterious. It's the only house that looks like this anywhere, I swear. Everything else is stucco this, McMansion that. But this place is just unique, you know? Thanks for letting me come over."

"As long as you're ready for disappointment," Lily said. "It really is gross. I saw this huge roach . . ."

But Rachel just waved that away. "It's Florida. Everybody has them. My mom has people come out to spray twice a month, and we still find them in the cabinets. That's why we call them palmetto bugs. To make them sound fancy. Even if they're gross."

While they were outside, Lily gave her a tour, showing her the locked door under the stairs, the bird feeder graveyard, the nasty dead pool, and the actually pretty interesting garden. They pulled down lemons right off the tree, but when they cut them open with their thumbnails, the fruit inside was pale and desiccated, and when they dared each other to taste them, the acid burned their tongues. Rachel said the pineapples were still too small to harvest, and neither girl was interested in the grapefruits.

Rachel looked at the pool like it was actually interesting. "So this is what happens if you don't take care of your pool," she said. "I bet you guys get some awesome frogs in there. Have you seen any cool birds?"

All of Lily's insecurities about having Rachel over to visit melted away. The girl was clearly thrilled to find the silver lining in every weird offering that was on hand. She told Rachel about the big, dinosaur-like birds she'd seen in the yard one morning, acting out their odd way of walking, hopping, and flapping their wings, and Rachel launched into every fact she knew about sandhill cranes.

They went inside and made sandwiches and ate them at the counter. Lily told Rachel about what the house had looked like when they first arrived, how you couldn't see a single square inch of floor, and how the entire den had been so full of garbage bags and boxes that you couldn't walk a straight line through it. Rachel asked if Lily had taken pictures, and Lily only then realized she hadn't. What would be the point? Dad had already bought the house—it wasn't like they could return it with the receipt just because they had proof that it sucked. Did they really have to think about how gross it had been?

But wait. She did have a couple of pictures—of her ruined bedroom. Not that she was going to show them to Rachel and freak her out.

As Lily showed Rachel the rest of the house, feeling less like an inhabitant and more like a tour guide of some bizarre roadside attraction, she couldn't help thinking about what Rachel would say if she told her about all the strange things that had happened to her here. The photos in the toilet. The way the bathroom water had turned green-black and splashed out onto the carpet. The spiders in the laundry room, and the crawling thing in the boxes, and the whispering shadow, and the jingling collar in her room. Not to mention the way that her bed had been tossed and the strange writing that had been left on the mattress.

She wanted Rachel to like her, not think that she was completely nuts, but . . . Well, Rachel was the one who'd brought up the caution tape and the ghost in the rain. And Rachel seemed pretty fascinated by the house's eccentricities. Lily wanted to trust her, wanted someone to share all her experiences and fears and secrets with, but she kept chickening out. She was fine with being called a drama queen, but only when she was being dramatic on purpose—not when she was actually scared out of her mind.

Lily was putting the plates in the dishwasher after lunch when she heard the snap of a phone camera. She looked up and caught Rachel guiltily putting her phone back in her pocket.

"What are you doing?"

Rachel looked down, uncertain. "Don't think this is weird, but I like watching ghost hunter shows, and I was taking a photo to see if there were any orbs or flashes. Like"—she looked up again and met Lily's gaze—"to see if there were any ghosts?"

"Why?" Lily felt like she was holding her breath, waiting to hear Rachel's answer.

Rachel chewed on her lip. "I mean, don't take this the wrong way, but I have a super-weird feeling. Like I'm being watched. Or is that crazy?"

Relief flooded Lily, just to know that Rachel was reaching the same conclusions. For the first time in days, she could draw a full breath. It made her feel stronger and more certain, finally having someone else confirm that this place was definitely not normal.

"Actually, some really creepy stuff has been happening," Lily finally admitted. "If you want to hear about it?"

Rachel's eyes lit up and she leaned in. "Yes. Please. I love scary movies, but I've never been anywhere haunted before. Tell me everything."

So they went back outside to walk around where Lily's mom wouldn't overhear, and Lily told her everything. The green eyes, the scrawled words, the black water, the child-shaped thing, the nightmare. *Everything.* Lily even showed Rachel the pics on her phone of her tossed room and those threatening words on the mattress. She kept looking to Rachel to make sure she wasn't just getting set up for ridicule, but Rachel seemed to be taking it very seriously and asked her tons of questions about ghost stuff—cold spots, objects moving around, electrical problems.

"Have you checked under your mattress lately?" Rachel finally asked.

Lily's fingertips went cold and numb. "Uh, no. Too worried about what I'll find." She looked back at the house, poking up at the bright blue sky like a broken brown tooth. "So . . . you believe me?"

Rachel looked at the house, too, her head cocked. "Yeah, why wouldn't I? It all adds up, doesn't it? And . . . I mean, it really does feel like we're being watched. Right? Like eyes on the back of your neck."

Lily did feel it—she always felt it here. "Do you want to leave? We can do something else."

Rachel grinned at her. "No way. I want to go see your mattress. If that's not weird. I bet ghost-hunting equipment would go crazy here. Maybe you could set up your phone to record sounds overnight and see what happens."

If there were whispers or groans or whatever at night, Lily definitely didn't want to hear them, and her parents would just accuse her of making any noises herself, but she wasn't going to tell Rachel that. If Rachel wanted to see her bed, that was just fine. And if there was something written there?

Well, at least someone would finally believe her.

They went inside, and as they headed upstairs to Lily's room, Rachel stopped four steps up.

"Did you feel that?" Rachel asked.

Lily stopped, too. "Feel what?"

"The way that step jiggled. I bet this house has secret hidey-holes all over it. Have you checked for loose floorboards?"

"I did in my room. I didn't find anything." Lily didn't mention that, although she'd been kind of sad not to find anything at first, now she was glad to know there was no creepy hole in her room. But as for the stair . . .

"Which one?"

Rachel stepped two steps lower and squatted down to wiggle the board she'd been standing on. "This one. I could be wrong, but it feels loose. My grandmother in Savannah lives in a house like this, and they have a loose stair, and a hidden library, and all sorts of weird stuff. Doesn't this house feel old to you? Like, older than most houses around here? You just don't see a lot of wood houses here."

Lily ran her hand over the top of the loose board and couldn't help being curious. Maybe the little key to the cupboard under the stairs would be there, or maybe something even cooler, like Britney's diary. At least if something weird happened, there would be a witness. And it was daylight, too, not nighttime in between horrific nightmares.

Just as Rachel had guessed, the board wiggled loose and Lily was able to lift it up. The stair was hollow, making a neat little wooden box. And inside it was something seriously dramatic, something utterly enthralling.

It was a Ouija board.

16.

"OKAY," RACHEL SAID, SOUNDING UNSURE. "THAT'S A BIT MUCH."

Lily was surprised by her worry, considering Rachel had brought up ghosts. "It's kind of cool, though, right? I mean, a séance! Dramatic lighting, velvet robes, harpsichord music . . ."

If they'd found it at night, Lily would've been scared. If it had been covered with bloodstains or cobwebs—or worse, both—she would've thrown it in the swamp. But here it was, looking cleaner and newer than pretty much anything else in the house. Even if the thing made her stomach do backflips, Lily couldn't help being drawn to the drama of it all.

It was just a board game. Just paper and plastic.

Not shadows, not whispers, not the jingling of a collar.

Just a game—and one she knew well. She'd played with a Ouija board before at slumber parties, and she was definitely the person who took control and made it say all sorts of creepy stuff. If there was any magic behind such things, it was someone like Lily who wanted to make her friends either giggle or pee their pants.

Rachel stepped up one more stair like she was trying to get away from it. "I've heard they're evil."

"Evil? It's a board game. You can buy it from Amazon." Lily didn't want Rachel to think she was a complete dork, but then again, she needed Rachel to be here while she used it. If something crazy was going to happen, she didn't want to be alone.

"I don't know. Ghost hunting is one thing, but actually talking to a ghost, getting its attention . . ."

"It'll be fun," Lily said. "We can ask it about what happened here that night you saw all the lights. If there are ghosts, this will tell us for certain, right?"

Rachel sat and considered the open step. "I guess. I mean, it doesn't sound like a nice ghost, though. Everything you've said— It wants you to go away. Like, it wants to hurt you. I don't know if I want it to get mad at me, too."

Lily looked down at the box that was still lying in the hidden stair. It had been waiting under the wooden step for who knew how long, and yet there was no dust on it. But maybe there wasn't even a Ouija board in that box. Maybe it was something normal. Like Scrabble. There was no world in which Scrabble was scary.

"But . . ." Lily paused, considering. "Don't you want to know, either way?"

It was a dare, plain and simple.

Their eyes met as Rachel considered it, lips twitching. She tentatively picked up the box, put it in her lap, and opened it as if it was the most normal thing in the world to find a Ouija board under a hidden stair in the creepiest house in Florida.

"It has everything," Rachel confirmed. "Even the little triangle thingy. The planchette, it says it's called. I think that's all we need, right?"

"I think so."

"I've never done it before. Can anything bad happen?" Rachel's natural curiosity was clearly warring with the freakiness of the house.

"Depends on what movies you watch and which books you read," Lily said. She was actually a little worried now that they were preparing to use the thing, but she had to pretend she wasn't scared. Rachel was here and the sun was out, and she wanted answers. Maybe, just maybe, the Ouija board could tell her something real about what she was experiencing.

"Oh, I watch plenty of horror movies, just none with Ouija boards," Rachel answered. "You have to come spend the night sometime soon. My house is extremely unhaunted. We can stay up all night watching scary movies and being terrified and eating candy."

Lily did not mention that she had spent several nights recently both awake and terrified, and she would not have enjoyed it, even with candy. She didn't really want to watch someone else going through it, either. Spooky books were more her speed, so she could put the story down and walk away when it got too intense. But she didn't want to tell Rachel that, not now.

Rachel stood holding the box in her hands. "So should we do this in your room? Or maybe out on the dock, since that's where I saw the caution tape?"

Neither spot sounded like fun. Lily's room sometimes had a life of its own, and the rickety, slimy dock down by the deep, dark water always made her uneasy.

"My room, I guess," she decided.

The steps had never seemed particularly challenging before, but now each one felt like it was a yard tall. Lily wanted to do this, or at least she wanted answers, but that didn't mean she wasn't scared.

Luckily, she was very good at pretending to be brave.

Lily led the way into her room, which looked normal enough, if a little sad and dull. Rachel didn't say anything about it, but she did look around briefly, her mouth pursed.

"My stuff should be here next week," Lily said, as sort of an apology. "I know it's pretty . . . drab."

At that Rachel looked around more carefully. "So everything that's here belongs to . . ."

"Yeah. Whoever lived here before." Lily wasn't quite ready to say Britney's name out loud. It would be a good test of whether or not it worked when Lily wasn't moving the planchette: If they asked the Ouija board for a name, Rachel wouldn't be able to make it spell out the name she didn't know.

Rachel handed Lily the box, and Lily sat down cross-legged and spread out the board in front of her. "Now you sit down across from me, and we both put our fingertips very lightly on the planchette. Then we ask questions, and it gives answers."

Rachel sat down. "Does it give the answers, or do ghosts do it? Kyle said he did this once at a party, and there were like ten guys doing it at once, and David Bowie's ghost supposedly told them to run around the house in their underwear. I'm pretty sure it wasn't a real ghost, though." Rachel giggled nervously, and Lily tried to smile a normal smile, but for the first time, weirdly, her mouth had forgotten how.

She realized they hadn't checked under her mattress yet, and she glanced behind her door to make sure the shadows there weren't doing anything sinister. Which they weren't. Everything seemed calm and still. The usual afternoon thunderstorm was on its way, the sky just beginning to turn gray. Eventually the black clouds would roll in, and heavy rain would beat the house and lash at the trees. But for now, things seemed tranquil enough. And even the storm was just a normal part of Florida life.

Lily put her fingertips on the triangle thing—the planchette, she reminded herself. She gave Rachel a look, checking that she was still all in, and nodded at her in an encouraging, brave sort of way. Rachel put her fingertips on it, too. In the center of the planchette was a circular window, and Lily eyed it warily.

"What should we ask it?" Rachel said.

"Whatever you want." Lily had her own questions, but it would seem more natural if she let Rachel go first.

"Is there a ghost here?"

Rachel's voice was low and solemn and properly dramatic. Lily approved.

Her fingertips were cold on the planchette, and she was committed to not moving it herself. But she was also paying close attention and hoping that she would be able to tell if Rachel tried to move the light plastic object on her own. Lily was expecting something to happen, but she thought it would be slow and gentle, like the two girls were trying to convince each other. Instead, the planchette dragged their fingers quickly to the word *YES*.

Rachel did not giggle, which is what Lily had expected her to do. Instead, Rachel looked at her with wide, serious eyes. "Did you do that?"

"Definitely not. Did you? Did . . . we?"

She and Rachel were looking directly into each other's eyes when the planchette bucked underneath their fingertips again.

When Lily looked down, the planchette was pointing at the word *NO*.

So, no, neither girl was controlling the planchette, supposedly. Lily pressed down a little harder, just in case it was Rachel moving it, so that Rachel would know she was onto her.

"How many ghosts are here?" Rachel asked, almost a dare.

The planchette jerked over to *1* and then *2*, dragging Lily's fingertips with it.

Rachel looked at Lily, as if she had any idea what was going on. "Does that mean one or two? Or twelve?"

In a tiny whisper, Lily said, "Ask it for a name."

But Rachel didn't have to ask. The planchette jumped again, forcefully.

It landed on *B*.

Then *R*.

Then *I*.

Every hair on Lily's arms rose as she waited for the planchette to land on *T*.

But it didn't.

It landed on *A*, then *N*.

"Brian?" Rachel asked. "That's a weird name for a ghost."

YES, the planchette said again.

"Not Britney?" Lily asked. She wanted to be very sure. The planchette jumped to *NO* and remained there as if a magnet held it down. It began shaking like there was a bee inside it angrily buzzing, desperate to stay in that one place. In the next heartbeat, Lily remembered the prescriptions she'd found carefully clipped together in the laundry room.

Prescriptions for Brian Richardson.

"Did you used to live here, Brian?" Rachel asked.

YES.

"Did you die here, Brian?" Lily asked.

YES.

Lily looked up at Rachel again. Rachel's eyes were wide with either fear or excitement, and she was shaking. Lily tried to pull her fingers away from the planchette, but she suddenly realized that they were ice cold, her fingertips frozen to the plastic, stuck to it with that burning tug that felt like touching ice with wet hands.

Well, fine. If the board wasn't done with Lily, then Lily wasn't done with the board.

"How did you die, Brian?"

"Maybe we shouldn't—" Rachel started, but the planchette didn't care. It jumped from letter to letter, taking their fingers with it, swift and shaky, certain but also frightened.

GOT OLD HEART PROBLEMS DIDNT TAKE PILLS DIDNT SEE THE POINT AFTER

The planchette clung to the final *R* and gently quivered under their fingertips.

"After what, Brian?" Rachel asked softly.

Lily wanted to close her eyes. She wanted to yell at Rachel for finding the stupid stair and at herself for thinking that the Ouija board was a good idea. It wasn't funny or fun or cute. It was terrifying, and she wanted to pull away her fingertips and run downstairs to her mom, but she couldn't. She was stuck here, pinned in place. The planchette was shivering now, and the room began to go cold and dark, and the shadows swirled like fog in the corners and behind the door and under the bed.

In a different voice than the cool, commanding one she had used to speak to the Ouija board previously, Rachel whispered, "What's happening? I don't like this."

The planchette jerked under their fingers, as shaky as an old man's hands fumbling with the childproof cap on his heart medicine.

YOU DONE IT NOW, the planchette said.

"We did what?" Lily whispered.

Letter by letter, the planchette scurried across the board like a spider.

BRITNEY IS COMING.

17.

"WHO IS BRITNEY?" RACHEL ASKED.

Instead of answering, Lily stood up suddenly. If she couldn't let go of the planchette, then she would at least get it off that horrible, haunted board. But the planchette clattered to the ground and skittered under her bed like a roach. She kicked the board as hard as she could, and it flapped out the door and onto the landing by the stairs. Rachel was still sitting down, mouth hanging open and fingertips hovering over where the board and planchette had just been.

"I don't think we want to know," Lily said. "Come on. We have to get out of here."

When Rachel didn't immediately stand, Lily reached down and grabbed her hands, pulling her up.

"Why? Who is Britney? What does that mean—Britney is coming?"

Lily shook her head and pulled Rachel toward the door, but the door slammed shut in her face. The lights went out, but the ceiling fan turned on and began to twirl faster and faster until all four lightbulbs were rattling in their cups, the entire fan shaking like it was about to fall. The sick green light of the oncoming storm leaked through the blinds, making everything the color of zombie skin.

"Seriously, what is this? Do you have a brother? Is this some kind of prank? Did you plan this whole thing?" Rachel asked. She was still shaking but no longer with anything remotely like excitement.

When Lily didn't immediately answer, Rachel yanked her hands away and looked at Lily like she was a rabid dog that could no longer be trusted. The room went even darker, and the tree branches began to beat at the roof and walls, and then the rain fell like a bag of rocks. Lily couldn't even see outside anymore—it was dark as night. And just like last night, the room had gone colder than a walk-in freezer. Lily's skin prickled with goose bumps, and she realized that the stinging burn in her fingertips from when she released the planchette wasn't just the cold. When she looked down, several of her fingertips were dripping blood—the skin had been torn off.

A weird numbness began to creep down her arms, and she felt dizzy.

"I don't know what's going on," she said, unable to meet Rachel's eyes. "I just know we have to get out of here. Britney was . . . I mean, this was Britney's room. So I guess Britney is the little girl who . . ."

"Died," Rachel said in the tiniest voice. "So you're not doing this? This isn't, like, some drama thing?"

Lily held up her hands to show her bloody fingertips, and Rachel gasped.

"No, I'm not doing this."

Rachel ran to the door and yanked at the knob, but it didn't even budge. Lily could hear footsteps now coming slowly up the stairs. She wanted to believe that it was her mom coming to check on them after hearing the thump of the Ouija board and the slam of the door, but she knew better. The footsteps were too light and too slow. And with each one she heard a soft squelching noise. Her heart began to flutter, and her mouth went dry.

"I want to go now," Rachel whispered.

"Yeah, me too," Lily whispered back.

The footsteps stopped in front of the door. Lily stared at the gap underneath it, where there was half an inch of space be-tween the door and the floorboards. Would she see feet there, maybe Mom's ratty old socks? As she watched, water flooded under the door, dark and dirty, with green scum floating on top. The water smelled awful and looked like the water that she'd seen—or dreamed—in the downstairs bathroom. Lily and Rachel backed away toward the bed.

"Why did you call me?" an angry, high-pitched voice said.

It sounded babyish, like a spoiled little girl. "Why won't you go away? This is my room. Mine."

"Well, it's my room now!" Lily shouted back. The backs of her legs hit the bed, and she sat down heavily and scrambled back against the wall. "And I can't go away. My family lives here."

Thump!

It sounded like someone had kicked the door. Black water continued to flood in, rushing toward the bed in little waves.

"No! Mine! You can't ignore me! I'll make you see me!" The voice filled the room, putting pressure on Lily's ears and making her grit her teeth.

Rachel sat down, too, and reached for Lily's hand. They both stared at the door, clasped hands cold and shaking. Lily couldn't decide if she wanted it to stay shut . . . or to open and show her whatever this thing was, whatever Britney was. Was it worse to know or not know?

"You'll be mine, too . . ."

The voice trailed off, and then the room filled with mad laughter, a little girl's demented giggling.

Lily didn't know how to make Britney go away. Beside her, Rachel trembled, her eyes closed. So Lily did the same thing she'd done this morning, something that came very naturally: She closed her eyes and screamed bloody murder so hard that the back of her throat burned. And when she ran out of air, she took a deep breath and screamed again. Rachel joined her, and Lily was glad to have someone with her, to feel her palm pressed against Rachel's, even as her fingertips throbbed.

"Lily? What on earth?"

Lily stopped screaming and opened her eyes. Her mother stood in her doorway. There was no water on the floor, and the lamp was on again, and the fan was slowing to a standstill. The storm outside had fallen away to gray drizzle. Rachel had also stopped screaming; she swiftly pulled her hand away.

"Hi, Mom," Lily said, her voice scratchy and small.

"Care to explain why you two are sitting on the bed, holding hands and screaming for no good reason? You nearly gave me a heart attack!"

Lily felt a tiny wash of guilt at making her mom mad, but then again, there had been a very good reason for the screaming. It seemed to be the only thing that drove away . . . well, fine. She'd call it what it was.

The ghost.

Britney's ghost.

"We were just . . . ," Lily began. She looked at Rachel, who looked like she was in shock. With a deep breath, Lily put on a smile and said, "We were practicing our stage screams. I was teaching Rachel what I learned in Broadway camp. Sorry if we scared you."

Her mom's face went from exasperated to annoyed. "Well,

go outside if you want to make noise. Although I really wish you guys wouldn't scream like that—it makes every adult in the area have a panic attack. I swear, my heart is still pounding."

Mine, too, Lily thought.

Mom shook her head at them in that kids-are-so-silly way, then turned to leave.

Rachel hopped up and shakily said, "I should go."

Lily's heart fell. It had been a bad idea, letting Rachel come over to her stupid, creepy, haunted house. She was about to lose her first and only friend in the entire state of Florida, and it wasn't even her fault.

"No, wait," Lily said, standing up. "Please."

Mom was all the way down the stairs now, and Rachel looked at Lily like she'd been wounded.

"No offense. Like, I know it's not your fault. But that was weird. Your room is just . . . I need to go. I'll text you later." She shivered and frowned and played with her friendship bracelets, waiting for Lily to say something.

"Maybe we could go for a boat ride tomorrow?" Lily offered. "Or jump on the trampoline? I can just walk over, if you don't want to go on the boat."

Rachel smiled weakly. "Yeah, okay, whatever. Just . . . you come to my house next time. And no more Ouija board."

Lily wanted to remind Rachel that she was the one who'd

found the stupid thing in the first place, but she recognized a peace offering when she saw one. If Rachel never wanted to talk about ghosts again, that was fair, after what had just happened.

As Rachel walked toward the door, she kept looking back, like Lily needed to be watched carefully.

Lily followed her to the top of the stairs. "I'm sorry," she said. "That's not . . . That hasn't happened before. I don't even know what just happened. I only knew that this was Britney's room because her name is in some of the books."

Rachel shrugged. "Well, I guess we've learned a lesson about finding mysterious haunted Ouija boards in hidden secret stairs and using them to contact dead children." A strangled giggle burst out of her mouth, surprising her. "Oh my God, I can't believe I just said that sentence. This is nuts. Yeah, definitely going home now. Text me if it ever starts to make sense, or if you think we had some kind of shared, messed-up daydream or got poisoned by peanut butter sandwiches."

Lily laughed, too, and she couldn't believe that they were both laughing after what they'd just been through. The laughter seemed to help the fear drain away.

"Yeah, okay. Lesson learned," Lily said.

Rachel gave a sad little wave and turned to go.

But as she put her foot on the top stair, it was as if someone stepped out and shoved her. She squeaked and her arms pinwheeled as she floated in space for just a moment before tumbling, flailing down all fourteen steps with a series of sickening thumps.

As Lily watched from upstairs, Rachel landed on the floor of the den like a broken doll.

18.

THEY HAD TO CALL AN AMBULANCE. LILY'S MOM USED HER CELL PHONE, speaking quickly as she stumbled over their new address. Rachel was crying, but Lily's mom told her not to touch Rachel, that she had definitely broken her arm and could possibly have damaged her back or neck. Rachel begged Lily's mom to use her phone to call Kyle, and when Mom asked if Rachel wanted her to call her parents, too, Rachel muttered that they were in Greece and Carla would handle it, then went back to crying.

Kyle beat the ambulance to the door, and he practically shoved Lily out of the way to get to Rachel, even as Mom warned him not to touch her. An older woman sat in the driver's seat of the shiny Land Rover he'd leapt out of, glasses pulled down on her nose while she texted, frowning.

"Don't touch her? Screw that," Kyle said, scooping Rachel

up and hugging her to his chest as she really let loose with the sobs. "Where does it hurt, Rachy?" he asked in a soft voice.

She just moaned and answered, "Everywhere."

The wail of sirens cut through all the tears, and Mom stood in the open door, arms crossed, waiting to direct the EMTs.

Through all this, Lily just stood there, numb. She felt like she was watching things happen from someplace far removed, from the audience, like this was a play she'd seen before and wasn't a part of. There was no role for her, nothing to do. Rachel wouldn't look at her. Soon strangers in uniforms were rolling a gurney in and moving Rachel onto it as bright lights flashed in the yard and people talked into radios. Was this what it had looked like, Lily wondered, the night Rachel saw lights here?

"What happened?" someone asked Mom, and Mom just said, "I don't know. I wasn't there. She fell down the stairs."

When one of the EMTs asked if there had been witnesses, Mom pointed them to Lily, and they asked her so many questions that she started crying, too.

"I don't know, I don't know," she told them. "She was standing at the top of the stairs, and then she just fell."

One of the EMTs grabbed Lily's hand, and turned it over, looking at her bloody fingertips. With everything else going on, she had totally forgotten about the pain.

"What happened here?" he asked her, opening his kit and gently swabbing her skin with a sharp-smelling pad. He had a bushy beard, a deep Southern accent, and kind eyes.

"I don't know," she moaned, shivering at the sting of whatever he was using.

"You tellin' me you don't know how you ripped off four of your fingertips?"

She shook her head, and closed her eyes, wishing for the pain to go away, and for Rachel to be okay, and for her house to be a place that felt good and comfortable and safe.

"We were playing with a Ouija board," she managed. "It . . . it got weird."

The EMT dabbed ointment on her fingertips and wrapped each one gently with a Band-Aid. "I'm not supposed to do this," he said, "so we'll keep it our secret. But maybe don't go playing with that sort of scary stuff, okay? Looks like it got out of control."

They were rolling out Rachel's gurney now, and Kyle was right beside his sister. Lily nodded at the EMT and murmured a thank-you before following the gurney out the door.

"Are you okay?" she asked Rachel.

Rachel had stopped crying. She was strapped down and had an IV in her hand with several bags dripping into it. Her smile was wide and wobbling, her pupils huge.

"I'm fine," she said. "Doesn't hurt anymore."

It came out all slurry, and Lily figured she was on some kind of medicine for pain.

"You're not fine. You've got several fractures," Kyle said. He pinned Lily with a glare. "You stay away from her, you hear me? Freaky kid, running out of the swamp. You let this happen to her!"

Lily jerked back like he'd slapped her. "Me? I didn't do this!"

"She's right," Rachel said, frowning and confused. "Wasn't her. It was Britney."

"Who's Britney?" Kyle asked.

"The girl in the rain."

"The what?"

But Rachel just turned her head away on the paper pillow, her eyes closing. They put her gurney in the back of the ambulance, and Kyle jumped in and shot up his middle finger at Lily as the doors closed.

The emergency vehicles pulled away, lights on and sirens off, and Lily just stood on the wet gravel and watched, feeling sick with guilt. Warm arms encircled her, and Mom hugged her from behind.

"She's going to be okay, sweetie," she said.

"Maybe," Lily replied. Right now, it felt like nothing would ever be okay again.

"She just slipped. It was an accident."

Lily took a deep breath. "No, Mom. It was a ghost. Our house is haunted."

There was a long, expectant pause, and her mom sighed sadly, her chin on Lily's shoulder.

"I know it's your thing, but let's not be dramatic about something this serious. Old houses can be creepy, and I know you don't like it here yet. But you can't blame this on ghosts. Rachel is just a little girl who went down some old wood stairs too fast in her socks. We probably need to get some carpet put down so it doesn't happen again." Mom pulled away. "Oh God. Do you think her parents are going to sue us? *Can* they sue us for that? I've got to call your father."

Mom hurried inside, leaving Lily alone in the driveway. Standing there, she could feel the blood pulsing in her bandaged fingertips. Were they burned? Frozen? Torn? She hadn't really looked; she just knew they were bleeding. Carefully she peeled back one of the Band-Aids.

All she saw was blood.

19.

DINNER WAS QUIET THAT NIGHT. LILY COULD TELL THAT HER PARENTS were nervous about Rachel's fall. Her mom's phone was out on the table, and both her parents kept glancing nervously at the door, waiting for Rachel's angry parents—or their angry lawyers—to knock. But nothing happened. Lily barely tasted her food, and no one asked her about her four identical Band-Aids—well, five, considering the accident with the scissors. She longed for the comforts of Wi-Fi and full bars, of being able to distract herself with stupid memes or a cozy Disney movie marathon. There were about a dozen things she needed to Google. But all she had was her barely functional phone, which was only good for talking and texting—and sometimes not even that.

Lily's parents disappeared to their room after dinner, and hearing them argue through their closed door was about the only thing in the world more uncomfortable than sharing her room with an angry ghost. She put away the dishes herself and went upstairs, careful to hold the railing tightly. She was surprised to find the Ouija board still upside down at the top of the stairs, and for now, she carefully stepped over it and left it there.

The lamp in her room was still on, everything exactly as it had been when Rachel fell. On hands and knees, she found the planchette under her bed and swept it out using one of Britney's books. She put socks over her hands before she returned the Ouija board and planchette to their box and put the top on it—she definitely wasn't going to touch any of it again with her skin. Sitting on her butt, she scooted down the steps one by one, put the board back in the secret stair, and refitted everything so it looked totally normal. If she'd had superglue or a hammer and nails, she would've made sure no one else could get that Ouija board out of its hiding place ever again.

Back in her room, Lily walked around nervously. It didn't feel safe. It didn't feel like home. It felt like Britney's place, like Britney could come back anytime and do something horrible. But downstairs felt no better, and she couldn't imagine trying to fall asleep on the old, musty couch. She was so exhausted and sleepy she could hardly stand, but she was filled with nervous energy. She couldn't even do the math to figure out how long she'd gone without a full night's sleep.

She wasn't sure what to do, but she had an idea and figured it might be worth a try. She pulled a blank page out of one of Britney's books, picked up a pen, and wrote,

> *Dear Britney,*
>
> *I'm sorry that you are angry. My parents said this was my room, so I have to live here now. Maybe you're the one who should go away. You don't belong here, and you're hurting people. Please leave us alone.*
>
> Signed,
> Lily

She left the note on the floor by the door and hoped it would be enough.

When she finally curled up in bed under her comforter, now stained with rusty-red drips from her fingertips, Lily didn't think she'd ever fall asleep. But the horrors of the day had used up all her energy. She nodded off almost immediately.

Her dreams were strange and very real. It was almost like she was awake as she threw off the covers, then snarled and pulled the comforter and sheets off the bed, hurling the pillows with all her might and stomping on the pile of fabric. She found the note by the door and sank her teeth into it, ripping it to shreds with her mouth and hands.

She walked down the center of the stairs, unafraid of

falling, unlocked the front door, and went outside. The moon was a Cheshire Cat grin high in a cloudless sky, and she smiled at the stars and identified Orion's belt and Sirius and the Big Dipper. She put two fingers between her lips and whistled, and a joyous bark sounded in the forest. Soon Buddy came running with a new confidence, his tail wagging like a flag as he leapt up and put his paws on her, then frisked around and rolled on the ground, showing his belly for tummy rubs. She knelt and patted him all over and accepted his frantic licks before standing again and looking out toward the lake.

The gravel hurt her bare feet, but she didn't care. Walking toward the dock, she felt mosquitoes land on her and didn't slap them away. The humid air settled over her like a blanket, and she breathed in deep, smelling the lemons on the trees and the honeysuckle tangled in the forest, all of nature opening up to the night's heat like a million hungry mouths. It felt good being here. It felt like home.

She kept walking until she stood fearlessly on the dock. The old wood was wet and soft under her feet, and she curled her toes into it. She went to the edge and sat down, letting her feet slip into the blood-warm water. Buddy settled down and sat by her side. She rubbed his skull and watched a big turtle surface and splash in the still black lake. It was so peaceful, so comforting.

And then, suddenly, terrifyingly, everything went black.

Her eyes were stuck open, and her teeth clacked together, and she was falling, falling, falling through the deep black water. All around her, the water was churning up, muddy, opaque, thick, and something was pulling at her, pulling her down, scratching her face and arms. But she couldn't fight it, couldn't move.

She just sank, sank, sank to the bottom of the deep, dark lake where all was still and black and she couldn't even open her mouth to scream.

And then the dream ended.

20.

WHEN SHE WOKE UP THE NEXT MORNING, LILY WAS ASLEEP ON TOP OF her comforter and sheets on the floor, covered in mosquito bites, and her feet were wet with mud. When her mom asked her why the front door was wide open, she had no idea.

She couldn't remember her dreams.

And the note she'd left for Britney was gone.

21.

WITH CJ AWAY AT CAMP AND RACHEL NOT ANSWERING LILY'S TEXTS, the days were long and boring. She read and crocheted and made friendship bracelets despite the fact that she now had no one to give them to. No matter where she was or what she did, Lily felt like the world was holding its breath, just waiting to exhale. Sometimes she thought maybe she was being watched, but when she spun around to look behind her, no one was there. She would take food outside whenever she felt lonely and call out for Buddy. She had never been able to whistle between her fingers before, but now she could, and anytime he heard her whistle, he came running. She had dreams of floating in blue water and woke up wishing her pool was clean.

One time, she fell asleep on the couch in the afternoon and woke up on her belly on the dock, her fingers trailing in the water. She tried to convince herself she'd been sleepwalking, but even her increasingly wild imagination couldn't fabricate a realistic story for why she would go there. She began subtly shoving chairs against the front door before she went to sleep, hoping that it would stop happening. She didn't tell her parents, though; it was exhausting being called overly dramatic when overly dramatic things were happening against one's will. It felt as if she were drifting through the days, floating on a lazy river, propelled by something outside herself.

One morning, when Buddy wasn't scared of her anymore and her mom was out shopping, she found an old bucket and took it outside. She filled it with hose water and added a squirt of shampoo and whistled. Buddy came running, and when he saw the hose, he wriggled with happiness and tried to bite the water. As long as she kept feeding him bits of food, he stood still enough for the bath. The fur that was revealed was a soft golden brown, and when she rinsed out the dirt and sticks and tangles that she had not yet cut out, it curled up. He looked like a real dog, like a well-loved dog, like a dog that any mother might welcome into her house, if he promised not to pee on anything. Lily still hadn't found his lost collar, and she had to assume her mother had thrown it away. When she ran out of food, Buddy bounced off into the forest, back to wherever it was he spent most of his time. He wouldn't come back no matter how much she whistled, so her hope of convincing her mom to let him come inside crumbled.

With nothing to do and the days gone long and hot, Lily took to reading more of Britney's books off the shelf in her room. They were all fantasy books, epic tales of magical realms where children had great powers and were often the key to saving the world. She hadn't liked this type of book so much before, had thought them frivolous and silly. She had enjoyed more realistic books about real kids with real problems—and, of course, anything about drama kids in particular. But now that *she* had real problems, the escape into fantasy was welcome. It was strange, though. There seemed to be fewer books than she remembered. The shelves had been crowded when she'd arrived, and now there was so much room that some of the books had fallen sideways.

With the house mostly cleaned out, her mom started going to work at the urgent care place just a few miles away. Part-time at first, so Lily often woke up in the morning to an empty house. She drifted from room to room, feeling like something was missing. Their storage container had gotten lost, so they didn't have their desktop and TVs. Even though the Wi-Fi and cable now worked, there was no way to use it. Her parents kept strict child locks on her phone, so she had texting and phone calls and music, but that was it. Bored to death, she found an old fishing rod in a trunk by the pool and caught bluegills from the dock with little balls of bread. Summer spread out, hot and slow, as summer tended to do.

A week passed, then two. The container was always supposedly on its way but never arrived. Lily began to think that all their belongings had been lost for good, that she would never again see her furniture or clothes or books. It was almost like they were stranded on a tiny island, out in the middle of the swamp. They couldn't see their neighbors' houses, and no one ever came down the long gravel driveway. Even the mail hadn't shown up yet. School was a month away, and she had no idea where she would be going; when she asked, her mom said the schools were weird here and she was waiting to see where Lily had been accepted. It was so easy to feel unmoored, so disconnected from real life. She'd never felt this way in Colorado.

Lily tried texting Rachel several times but got no response. She asked casual questions at first, then apologized for what had happened, then begged forgiveness. Finally, when she was so lonely she wanted to cry, she told her mom she was going for a walk, and she put on her old sneakers and headed out the same way she'd gone the day she'd ended up in Rachel's backyard. But she couldn't make her way through the sucking mud, protruding roots, hanging vines, and interlaced branches. She was hot, her skin prickling, her hair straggling into her eyes, and it seemed she had barely gone ten feet before her path was solidly blocked. She went back home and took a shower to wash the scent of the swamp off her skin.

That night, Lily again dreamed that she was swimming.

But this time the dream was more immediate, more real. She had never swum much in real life, outside of paddling around in a hotel pool once for CJ's birthday. She had hoped to learn to swim now that she lived in Florida. But if Rachel wouldn't return her texts, clearly she wouldn't be learning how to swim in Rachel's nice pool, and there was no way she'd put so much as a toe in the lake.

But in the dream? She swam like an otter, like she had always known what to do in the turquoise pool. It was wonderful. The water was silky and cool, and her hair floated out like a mermaid's. She could even flip forward or backward. She sank down, down, down to the bottom of the deep end and looked up at the shimmering corona of the sun. It was the nicest dream she'd had since moving to Florida, and she wanted it to go on forever. The sky was blue and the sun was warm and Lily floated on her back in crystal blue water, looking up at the string of Christmas lights that would shine at night in cheerful red, blue, and green. She felt at home and at peace.

Until everything changed.

The sky went dark like ink drops spreading in water. The pool was cold and clammy, the water growing viscous and thick, and her bones became leaden. Her feet touched down, scraping something hard, and her hair felt heavy, pulled underwater by invisible hands. She began to choke and thrash, trying to remember how to float, how to breathe, how to bring back the blue skies and the warm sun. But the darkness could not be repelled.

In that moment, she realized this had to be a dream, one that was swiftly becoming a nightmare. So she did what had always worked before: She screamed and screamed and screamed. But instead of waking up, instead of feeling her mom's warm hand on her shoulder, she coughed and gasped as the thick black water ran down her throat, choking her. When she opened her eyes, everything was dark, except for a strange glimmer, a silver glow that seemed to touch every surface—and three colorful lights.

She wasn't in bed. She wasn't in her room. She wasn't even in the house.

She could feel the weight of the air outside, that heat that wrapped around her, thick and heavy as an old wool coat. She was wet and struggling, and she wasn't quite drowning, but she was standing in water somehow and . . .

Oh no.

Oh no oh no oh no.

It couldn't be.

Not this.

Lily was in the swimming pool.

Her swimming pool, the one in her yard, that nasty hole in the ground just brimming with muck.

She was on her tiptoes in the deep end, and the water would

choke her if she couldn't keep her nose and mouth above it. She knew that if she could only get to the shallow end, she would be okay. That part was dry, and there were steps that led up to the patio. In her dream she had known how to move, how to swim, how to use the water. But this was no dream, and this was not clear water. This was nasty green sludge choked with algae and plants and dead things, and she could feel them moving past her and brushing over her skin as she fought her way to safety. She tried screaming again, but the filthy water ran down her throat, making her splutter. Not like her mom could hear her all the way outside, anyway.

There was nothing to hold on to, nothing but her body and the water, which pushed against her like something living, like some monster that wanted to hold her close. She struggled against it, walking on the tips of her toes, pulling her arms through the swampy black liquid, so close to being able to pull her body up onto the dry, safe concrete, when her foot tripped on something that might have been a stick or a snake or an old, wet bone. It rattled under her foot, and she slipped, and her head went under the water.

She held her breath and flapped her arms, momentarily suspended as she struggled to find her feet again. There was nothing as dark as this place, nothing as terrifying as being trapped under that thick green water. Finally, she put down a foot and then another and flung her arms back, using her whole body to flounder up onto the dry concrete. Her fingers found it first, and her still-sensitive fingertips burned as she crawled on hands and knees up the steps. As soon as her entire body was out of the water, she flopped down on her side, pawing leaves and branches out of the way. A frog leapt into the air, terrified of her, and she almost laughed.

The thought that *she* was the scary thing here was hilarious.

She coughed up some vile black gunk and lay there, catching her breath. She was in her pajamas, soaked through. She had never been more exhausted in her life. Even covered in green slime, she felt like she had a fever, it was so hot out.

It took everything Lily had to drag herself to her wobbling feet and stagger away from the pool. Wiping gunk out of her eyes, she saw the kitchen door hanging open. Wearily she walked back toward the house, wincing as she stumbled over rocks and sticks and sharp, tiny shells. All the lights were out except for those three remaining Christmas lights hanging in the pool cage.

She paused at the doorstep.

If she walked inside right now, like this, she'd leave wet, slimy footprints everywhere, and then her mom would want to know what had happened, and she would be in trouble, or maybe end up in the psych ward somewhere. She'd read about insane asylums in a couple of horror books, and even though they couldn't be as bad as the ones from the 1800s, she still didn't want to try to explain to some old guy in a white coat that she was apparently sleepwalking and that a ghost had pushed her friend down the stairs.

With a heavy sigh, she reached into the kitchen and pulled over the roll of paper towels that sat by the stove. It was disgusting, rubbing wads of paper towels up and down her face and hair and arms and legs and seeing the white paper come away coated with green-and-black stains and peppered with dead bugs and rotten leaves. When she'd cleaned off all that she could, she tossed the pile of paper towels into the dumpster that still hadn't been picked up, locked the kitchen door firmly behind herself, and headed into her bathroom.

Watching the green water slough off her body in the shower, she murmured to herself, "I think I'm going crazy."

22.

THE NEXT MORNING, LILY REMEMBERED ONLY BITS AND PIECES OF
what had happened in the night, as if it really had been a
dream. But the pile of green-and-black-smeared paper towels
in the dumpster did not lie. After breakfast she walked outside
to the dented and ripped pool cage and stood over the still,
thick, murky water. A green-black smear stretched from the
water to the stairs, where her footprints were clearly visible.

It definitely wasn't a dream.

Hands shaking, she brought a bowl of water from the
kitchen and scrubbed the footprints away with more paper
towels. Her parents never came out here, but she couldn't take
the risk.

That day books could not hold her attention, and wherever
she went, she felt jumpy. Her mind was as dark and twisty
as the pool water. Was she going crazy, or was there really a

ghost—or two ghosts—haunting the new house? Neither answer was good. And thinking about it, trying to figure out
which one was worse, was making her even crazier. Horrible
thoughts spun through her head, thoughts of drowning or falling down the stairs or having her legs chopped off by the fan.
She felt lost in her own life with no safe harbor and no one she
could trust. She quietly murmured, "Beetlejuice, Beetlejuice,
Beetlejuice," like in the musical, but no one showed up from
the other side to offer helpful suggestions.

As a last-ditch effort to distract herself, she decided she
needed something to do, if only to stop her hands from fidget-
ing and her imagination from taking her down terrifying paths.

Her mom was at work, so Lily decided to poke around.
After all the cleaning, it had been a relief to spend a few days
without putting on yellow gloves or touching garbage bags,
but it occurred to her that no one had yet tackled the spare
room downstairs. Her mother had taken one look, firmly closed
the door, and said, "We've got the dumpster for a while yet.
This can wait. Not like it's going anywhere."

Now Lily gathered up a pair of gloves and a roll of garbage
bags, and for the first time she stepped into the room that was
so horrible even her mother had shied away.

It was even more densely packed than the den had been,
but it looked like everything shoved into the spare room had
been important—to someone, at some time. This wasn't regular

garbage but the sort of stuff old people accumulated over a lifetime, things too special to throw away, but only special to them. Trunks, boxes, thick brown folders of files held together with twine. Somewhere under all of it, she could see a dresser and the wooden posts of an old bed.

Her mouth twitched up. This room might actually hold the clues to what had happened to Brian and Britney. Well, if the Ouija board was right, Brian had died because he'd neglected to take his medicine, but she still had no idea what had happened to Britney. It would be ridiculous if what she needed to know had been sitting in here all along. As a bonus, her parents would probably be really pleased with her for doing some cleaning on her own and making the house more livable.

She put on her gloves and stepped inside. Closest to the open door were boxes stacked and labeled with things like *Photos* and *Taxes* and *Barbara's China*. Those boxes were too heavy for Lily to lift, so she slipped around them to see what else was on the bed and dresser.

The first interesting thing she found was an old photo album. There was no label on the outside of the book, but as she flipped through it, she could see notations in careful, faded handwriting. She stopped when one caught her eye. *Brian holds Melissa for the first time,* it read. The man in the picture was holding a baby wrapped in a pink blanket, smiling for the camera. The photo was old, like from the eighties.

"Brian," Lily murmured to herself.

But who was Melissa?

The album showed Melissa going from a baby to ten years old, with pictures of her swimming in the ocean, or roller-skating, or learning to ride a bike as Brian ran behind her. Every now and then, rarely, a woman showed up in the pictures. She was younger than Brian, smiling and pretty. And then the book ended with Melissa at a restaurant for her tenth birthday party, with some creepy animatronic mouse looming behind her in striped overalls. The next album Lily found started with Melissa in a uniform, going to school. There was a Christmas picture, where Melissa got an old-fashioned Nintendo. And then there was a picture of crying Melissa hugging her mother, who was in a bed in the hospital. And then the album ended abruptly, leaving many empty pages.

Lily looked around for another album but didn't find one. What had happened to the woman, and why were there no more pictures of Melissa? And where did Britney fit into the picture?

She focused on the box labeled *Photos*. It was full of paper, but she didn't see any actual photos. There were hundreds, maybe thousands of Amazon packing slips. She used a nearby pencil to move the papers around, but the box was just too deep to see if there was anything interesting underneath, and she was still too skittish about the idea of roaches and spiders to dig around.

Oh well. Maybe if she cleaned up some of this junk, she would find more clues. She opened one of the black bags and began cleaning obvious garbage off the table. There were more receipts, plus stacks of magazines on fishing, hunting, and guns, with some old *Highlights* magazines mixed in. Under the table, she found boxes full of clothes, all for a little girl, in sizes six and seven. She thought about saving them for the donations bin, but they were faded and covered in roach eggs and mouse poop, so she carried them out to the dumpster. She threw away boxes of chewing tobacco and cigars, plastic bags filled with rags and paintbrushes rock-hard with yellow paint. She saved an old tool kit and a tackle box full of fishing stuff. She threw away broken toasters and plastic plates and a huge box full of old Christmas lights like the ones hanging around the pool cage. The ancient artificial tree went to the trash, too. She was getting lots of exercise, running to and from the dumpster again.

A little after noon, her mom showed up to grab her for-gotten lunch. Apparently Lily had missed her text while she'd been cleaning, and she nearly had a heart attack when the front door opened. Lily didn't want her mom to see the spare room until it was clean, so she shut the door and tiptoed in from the den. As they ate their sandwiches, Lily looked up and chose her words carefully.

"Mom, do you know when—"

With a snort, her mom interrupted her, which she didn't do

very often. "No, I don't know when the storage container will get here. Believe me, it's making us all crazy."

So Lily tried a different tack. "Could you maybe unlock the internet on my phone? I'd at least like to look up the schools I might end up going to."

Much to her surprise, her mom put her head in her hands and moaned. "Look, I know. I know I need to figure it out. I need to figure everything out. I'm trying, but it's wearing me so thin. This place is getting to me."

It felt like all noise ceased. That constant outdoor hum of bugs and birds went silent. The skin prickled up the back of Lily's neck.

"Me too," she said quietly.

Her mom looked up, worry in her eyes. "Yeah?"

"Nightmares," Lily said, looking down. "Like, a lot. And Rachel."

Her mom put a hand on her arm. "Honey, I told you. That wasn't . . . She just slipped, okay? I saw the Ouija board at the top of the stairs. She slipped on it and fell. I'm sorry she's not talking to you, but no one could blame you. You're just a kid. It's not your fault if she's clumsy."

"She's not . . . I mean, that wasn't what happened."

Mom pulled away and gave her a bright-eyed look. "You're at a confusing age. Your brain and body are changing—"

"Mom! Stop! Gross!"

"I just need to remind you that . . . it's hard. I know it's hard. It's hard for everyone your age."

Lily gulped down a hysterical laugh. Most kids her age weren't waking up half drowned in abandoned swimming pools at midnight with no idea how they got there.

"It can make you feel cray, is all I'm saying. I definitely felt cray when I was your age."

Lily rolled her eyes. "Mom. Seriously. Don't say *cray,* okay?"

"Fine. Crazy. Out of control. Happy one second, angry the next. Crying for no reason. Insomnia, weird dreams, anxiety, depression, rage. Your body doesn't feel like your body anymore. You feel out of control. It's not just Florida—it's just part of being your age. Part of being you. And after what happened last year—" She broke off and smiled, so soft and full of pity. "I just know you have a lot of feelings right now."

Lily ignored that last bit and nervously picked the last chunk of her sandwich apart as she built up the nerve to ask her mom, "Do you believe in ghosts?"

But her mom just stood up to whisk the paper plates into the garbage. She was all work again, no nonsense.

"Of course not," she said a little too harshly. "I believe that when creative kids get bored, their imaginations go wild and they look for drama where there is none. But news flash: Most of life is just boring."

Lily got that deflated feeling she was becoming accustomed

to each time she tried to confide in her parents and was completely written off. Her mom had basically blamed all the freaky stuff that had happened on puberty and boredom. Which was just insulting. Weird mood swings did not make a kid sleepwalk into the pool. But whatever. She had known from the start that her mom wouldn't really hear what she had to say.

Mom went back to work, and Lily went back to the spare room to take her anger out on the junk taking up space in the house that was hers, whether she wanted it to be or not. She turned on the *Hamilton* soundtrack and got aggressive. She was not throwing away her shot, but she was throwing away pretty much everything else. At least most things were already in boxes that she could carry out to the dumpster. There were boxes of cloudy glass vases, boxes of used batteries dusted with acid powder, boxes of shoes so worn out that even the secondhand store couldn't use them. None of it was useful. It felt good to hurl it into the dumpster and hear it thump against the metal walls.

She had uncovered the entire spare bedroom now. All that was left was Barbara's china and the junk on the dresser. One thing caught her eye on the scarred, old wood, though: a set of keys with a mangy rabbit's foot on the key ring. That might actually be useful. Dad had not made good on his promise to have more keys made for the house.

Lily took the keys to the front door. As she had surmised,

the newest-looking silver key could lock and unlock it. There was also a car key, old and worn with a Toyota logo on it. One medium-sized key reminded her of the key for Rachel's boat. That made sense—maybe they used to have a boat here, too. And then she saw a small, heavy brass key. One that might be just the right size to open the secret door that led under the stairs.

As she walked outside, she definitely felt more fear than hope. After all, you didn't lock doors for no reason. She knelt, the gravel making dents in her knees as she considered the key and the lock.

Lily paused for a moment and took a deep breath. She had no idea what she would find behind the little door, but she suspected that it would not be good. Her neck tickled and her shoulders hunched with that now-familiar feeling of being watched, and she looked all around the yard. There was no one there that she could see—but there never was.

She swallowed her fear and put the key in the lock.

It fit perfectly.

23.

TIME SEEMED TO STOP. LILY'S KNUCKLES WERE WHITE AS SHE HELD THE key there without turning it. It occurred to her for the first time in her life that a lock, like a light switch, had only two positions. It was either closed or open, on or off. There was no in-between. Lily herself, on the other hand, felt like she was always somehow in-between.

She willed her fingers to turn the key in the lock, but she couldn't bring herself to do it. She could imagine so many horrible things behind that door—bodies and bones and clumps of tangled hair and coiled snakes writhing and thousands of spiders—and she was painfully aware that she was home alone. No amount of screaming would bring any sort of help.

A dog howled in the bushes, and she startled and pulled the key out of the lock. Buddy burst out of the forest, the fur raised along his back. He didn't look like a friendly, desperate goof just now. He was barking, growling, frothing at the mouth like he'd gone mad. Lily stood, clutched the keys in trembling fingers, and pressed her back against the house. Buddy advanced on her, walking stiffly, his head down at an unnatural angle as he growled.

"Hey, now, Buddy," she said, her voice low and calm. "It's just me. We're friends, right? We're buddies."

He didn't stop, and she looked frantically from side to side, hoping for some way to escape. But there was nothing she could climb, no door she could run through, just the flat sides of the house, the swamp, the deck, the flimsy screen door of the pool cage.

He barked, loud and shrill, and her fingers jerked open. The key ring dropped out of her hand and hit the ground with a *clunk*. Buddy lunged for her, and she kicked out as hard as she could, hating herself as she did it. Her foot met his soft body, and he yelped in surprise and—was it fear?

When she looked down, Buddy had the rabbit's foot in his mouth and was staring at her like she'd betrayed him. He whined softly, turned, and slunk back into the bushes with the key ring.

The beast that had been stalking her was gone, and her only remaining friend was abandoning her.

"I didn't mean to kick you, Buddy! I thought you were going to bite me! Come back. Please? I'll get you some pizza."

But the dog didn't turn around or even flick an ear. He had disappeared completely into the undergrowth with the jingling keys, his tail tucked between his legs and his head down.

Now he was ignoring her, too.

And the door under the stairs?

It was still locked.

24.

NOT KNOWING WHAT ELSE TO DO, LILY WENT BACK INSIDE AND CON-
tinued cleaning out the spare room. It was just work now,
just something she had to finish, and it had lost any appeal
or sense of adventure. She didn't need to dig into every box
and drawer looking for some secret answer to all the questions
around her. She'd found the keys she'd been looking for, but
they'd only made things worse. It felt like every choice she'd
made was the wrong one. The shame and guilt over Rachel's
accident had already been eating her alive before she'd kicked
Buddy. So now she would stop texting Rachel; she would stop
calling for Buddy. She didn't want to hurt them any more than
she already had.

By dinnertime the spare room was clean, and Lily's mom
unexpectedly gave her a big, warm hug and told her she was
proud of her. The dumpster company was scheduled to come
get the dumpster soon, and that was that. Maybe if she just

kept her head down and ignored the ghosts and their business, the ghosts would ignore her, too. Maybe her parents had been right. Pretend to be normal long enough, and you start to believe it yourself.

That night, everything seemed a little brighter. Lily's mom was in a good mood after a great day at work. Her dad's job was going well, and he actually seemed to be tuned in at dinner. Her mom had finally decided where Lily would be going to school and had printed out some info at work. There wasn't a drama club, but there was a spring musical and even a small stage in the cafeteria. Lily took all this good news as a sign. Things were going to be okay. Period.

She went to sleep feeling content and optimistic.

But when she woke up in the middle of the night, something was very, very wrong.

It was too dark.

The room felt crowded, full of rustling, looming shadows, the air thick with rot.

She wasn't in her bed.

Whatever she was lying on felt soft and damp and spongy.

Nearby, someone sighed.

And it wasn't either of Lily's parents.

She heard something move, heard a subtle click, and white-blue light filled the space as an old TV turned on to a dead channel. She was in the den downstairs, but it was full of towering piles of junk and garbage again, exactly the same as the day they'd moved in. The only difference was that the couch where she was lying was cleared off, and both of the big recliners were in their places, their backs turned to her. The stacks of boxes and bags loomed around her like the skeletons of a destroyed city. It felt like something out of a zombie movie, when there's nothing left of the human race but bones and rotting towers.

Someone cleared their throat, and one of the recliners slowly swiveled to face her with a rusty creak. Sitting in the chair, his face a collection of hideous crags and cracks in the shifting gray light, sat an old man.

The old man looked like he was dead.

His skin was thick and grayish, pulled tight over his bones and then hanging like melted wax. His eyes, perhaps once a bright blue, were opaque white and wet where they peeked out from under drooping eyebrows with long white hairs that waved in the air like antennae. He wore baggy pajama pants, a faded ball cap, and the sort of slippers everyone gave to grandpas they didn't know well. His white T-shirt was stained yellow like the ones she'd cleared out of the laundry room, but was stuck to his body by seeping patches that looked like pus. She wanted to scream and run away, but she was frozen in place. Her eyes were the only things she could move, but try as she might, she couldn't close them.

She knew immediately that this was Brian, the man from the photo album and the spirit that had spoken to her and Rachel through the Ouija board. Despite her terror and inability to move, he didn't feel mean, like he wanted to hurt her. He just seemed sad.

"Been waiting for you," he said, his voice gravelly and deep and tired, tinged with a Southern drawl and accented with a wheeze.

"You have?" she asked, as her tongue had finally come unglued from her mouth. She tried to scream, but no sound came out.

He shook his head. "Nice try, but screaming won't save you. We got to talk."

For several minutes they sat there in silence. The old man's eyes were dead white with no pupils, but it seemed like he was focusing on something far away. There was no sound except for the ever-present hum of the orchestra of frogs, bugs, and night birds that seemed to never simmer down in a Florida summer, and the quiet rustling of the bags and cardboard around her, kissed by roach feet and the soft, furry bodies of spiders.

"What's happening?" Lily finally asked.

The old man cleared his throat. It was a wet, sick sound, his breathing pained and moaning. "You got Britney all riled up," he wheezed. "And I can't control her anymore. Never could, really. That child is like an August storm. You think it's gonna be a nice, sunny day, but then everything goes real dark real fast, and you got no choice but to run for cover."

Lily didn't know what to say to this. She had never been accused—by a ghost—of upsetting another ghost, and she could no longer tell dream from real life.

"I'm sorry?" she tried.

He snorted. "Sorry ain't gonna make things better."

She tried something different. "You're Brian, aren't you?"

"Yeah. That's me." He nodded and adjusted his ball cap. The flash of scalp she saw underneath reminded her of rotten mushrooms caving in. "Now, I don't mind you-all being here. I reckon somebody's got to keep the place nice, no matter what Britney thinks. I was here a heck of a lot longer than she was, and it's my place. Built it with my own two hands. I liked it quiet, but I don't mind you folks. Britney's another story, though."

"What happened?"

Brian sighed heavily and resettled himself in the beat-up recliner. He didn't seem like he was in a hurry, but Lily was beginning to feel like something bad was coming. She glanced to the front door, but it was obscured by piles of paper and cardboard. She wanted to check to see if it was locked. Then again, she knew that no lock could stop the truly scary things in life.

"I don't like to talk about it," Brian went on. "Don't like

to think about it. But I suppose somebody has to know what happened here. I bought this house to retire to. My wife was long gone—cancer—and our daughter, Melissa, had run off real young, made some mistakes in her life. Figured it would be nice and quiet here—do a little fishing, float in the pool, die in peace some day."

He barked a laugh and blackish liquid leaked from the corner of his mouth.

"Which I did, outside of the peaceful part. But before that happened, the police showed up one day with a social worker and a little girl I'd never seen before, clutching a sad ol' stuffed pink bunny. Said she was my granddaughter, and I was her closest remaining relative. She was only six, undersized and scrawny little thing, all scared and twitchy, weird and angry. Turns out she was Melissa's kid and they'd been living out of her car, somewhere up in Georgia. Melissa got into some bad stuff and died, rest her soul, and so they came lookin' for me."

He paused to stare into the darkness like the news was on and he was waiting for the weather.

"So there I was, sixty-six and living off by myself for twenty years like a dang hermit when this messed-up little kid gets dumped on me. I didn't know what to do. It was hard, taking her out in public—her mama had made her odd. Didn't know how to act around people. She'd grab stuff she wanted and hiss if you tried to take it back. Real territorial. Never would let go of that dang bunny and wouldn't let me wash it. Filthy thing. But she needed stuff, and I had my computer, so I just started ordering clothes and whatever. It was just us and Amazon." He held out an arm and gestured to the room beyond, and Lily finally understood why the house was heaped in cardboard boxes.

"I sent her to school, but she was always in trouble. Couldn't cooperate, didn't want to do what anybody said. They put her in special needs classes, and she got better. Learned how to read and got good at it. Her teacher recommended I get her a dog, kinda like a helper. Something to love, some way to reach her. So we got Buddy." He reached down between his leg and the recliner and held out the now-familiar collar, the tags winking in the TV's gray light. "And it worked. She finally let go of her bunny to play with Buddy. He was a good boy. But he wasn't a trained dog, you know. He was just a friend. I thought I could count on 'im to keep an eye on her." He sighed sadly.

"One summer morning I woke up around eleven—I always slept in late—and she didn't come down for lunch. I hollered upstairs but she didn't answer. Even hobbled on up there, which was hard for me, with my knees, but she wasn't in bed. I checked all the rooms—it wasn't like this then. I kept up with the trash, put the boxes in the recycling like you're supposed to. Kept things clean. Even checked that little crawl space outside that she liked to play in. Nothing. Then I noticed Buddy standing out on the dock. Dog was dripping wet and staring at the water, barking and growling and whining."

Lily could feel the story going bad, and she wanted it to change, but it was like trying to stop an eighteen-wheeler barreling right at you at full speed. She'd felt this way back in Boulder, the night that everything had gone wrong, like she was starring in the play but someone else was directing, and they'd changed the ending on her mid-monologue. All she could do now was lie there, waiting, helpless to stop what was coming.

Brian took a deep breath, and his eyes blinked a few times and leaked a little fluid.

"I went on out, and there she was. Just a-floating in the lake, facedown, dead and still."

Lily tried to imagine what that would be like and couldn't. She had never seen a dead body—not counting Brian, right now—and had only been to one funeral. She pictured this old man and Buddy out on the dock on a summer morning, seeing . . . something truly horrible. She tried to speak, to offer condolences, but it was as if the dream had stolen her tongue again, or perhaps Brian's emotions overpowered everything else.

"I called nine-one-one, and they sent out ambulances and a fire truck and police, all that. I didn't know what had happened. It made no sense. The child swam like a fish. I taught her myself. She spent every day playing in that pool, back when it was shiny blue and pretty. She loved to sit on the bottom and hold her breath and look up at the sky." His voice was shaking now. "I know it sounds like she was trouble, and she was, but it wasn't her fault she was that way. I loved her, fierce critter that she was. When they fished her out of the water and put her in a body bag, I had me a heart attack. Keeled over right by the dock."

He exhaled like the hard part of the story was over.

"They took her to the morgue and me to the emergency room. Doctors gave me a bunch of prescriptions, told me I had to take better care of myself or I'd have another heart attack, a worse one. But that child took the last of my heart with her. I came back home and never saw a doctor again. Quit going out. Just ordered whatever I needed on the computer. Let things stack up. It was my time to go, nothing left for me here. I wanted to die.

"And I did. Right here in this chair."

He pushed the recliner up to sitting and put his feet on the floor, leaning forward to get Lily's attention. She was stuck to the couch, unable to speak, barely able to breathe. She felt like a broken doll, cracked and cold. The hairs along the back of her neck rose, and goose bumps raced up her arms and legs. Lightning flashed through the heavy white curtains, and thunder boomed, and Lily could feel the pressure in the air, bearing down as if something was coming. Coming to get her.

"But Britney don't rest so easy. And I'm sorry, but since she couldn't make you leave, she's got somethin' else in mind. And I can't help you."

Thunder boomed again. The lights went out. The TV went black.

The only sound was the doorknob turning.

25.

TERROR EXPLODED IN LILY'S HEART, AND SHE BOLTED TO HER FEET.
Whatever hold Brian's ghost had exerted over her was gone.
She was no longer frozen. Maybe, like with the Ouija board,
Britney had driven him away. Thanks to the darkness, Lily
couldn't see if the recliner was empty or not, but whatever was
left of him, Brian was on his own.

With the room pitch-black and still full of towers of newspaper and cardboard and garbage bags, Lily didn't know where
to go. If she tried to maneuver through the labyrinth, she
would knock things over, shove things—and make noises that
would lead straight to her. She wanted to hide, but she knew
that this place was Britney's more than her own, and wherever
she went, Britney would follow.

The door squeaked open.

"I told you to go away."

The voice came from the open door. Britney sounded so young but so hurt and angry. Lily almost answered her, almost apologized and promised she would leave, even though she had no way to make it happen. But if she spoke, Britney would know where she was. She dropped to her hands and knees on the dusty wooden floorboards.

"I told you to leave Buddy alone. But you kept trying to take my stuff. My dog. My room. *Mine.* So you're gonna be mine, too."

Quietly, Lily scurried over behind the recliner, which was closer to the door. She heard squelching footsteps crossing the boards. Her mind showed her images of a drowned little girl, purple lips and gray-white skin stretched and bloated. She imagined black holes where eyes should be, where crows and vultures had plucked away the squishy whites. She imagined hair laced over with algae and water weeds. Her breathing sped up, and her heart pounded, and she started to go dizzy and numb. She had never felt so hopelessly trapped.

"If you had gone away, I wouldn't have to do this." Britney sounded like a little girl about to punish her dollies, furious but also gleeful. "But now you're here, and I want you to play with me. We could swim again. Did you like swimming with me?"

Lily's brain was going a mile a minute. She had to figure out a way to escape. But where could she hide? This was Britney's world, not hers. This wasn't even her own nightmare. Then she had an idea. She reached up to feel around in the recliner, and there it was. Buddy's collar. She wrapped her fist around the jingling tags to silence them and threw the collar across the room, aiming for the hall that led to what was now her parents' bedroom.

Just as she'd hoped, the thing that was Britney lumbered in that direction, panting like an animal, each breath wet and desperate. Lily heard the sound of knees hitting the boards and fingernails scrabbling for their prize. While Britney was occupied with the old collar, Lily found the wall with her hand and scuttled along it toward the open door. She slipped outside, her back against the side of the house, and stood.

The moon lit the yard in tones of black and white. She had to get away, but every direction held its own dangers. To the left was the swamp, where she had encountered the snake and the pitcher plants that seemed full of blood. To the right was the caged pool filled with water that was black and murky. Straight ahead was the dock and the lake, the place where Brian had found Britney's body. Old ribbons of yellow caution tape floated in the nonexistent wind, torn and trembling, and wet footsteps glistened on the dock.

So Lily ran in a new direction, her bare feet stung by gravel and bits of shell and sticks. She ran toward the road. Branches and leaves plucked at her nightshirt, and strange noises echoed through the darkness, animalistic screams and howls. Soon she heard footsteps pounding on the gravel behind her. She sped up. The road had to be close, and surely there would be cars there, people going about their lives who could help her. She stumbled past the mailbox and onto the cracked black asphalt.

There were no lights, no cars. She could not hear engines or voices. She could not see the neighbors' houses. Over the roar of the Florida night, she heard only wet footsteps coming closer and closer, steady stomps sending the gravel flying.

This had to be a dream. In real life, there were always cars, motorcycles, streetlights, houses with warmly lit windows. So she did what had worked in the past: She screamed and screamed and screamed until it shredded her throat. She screamed so loud that she couldn't hear the footsteps or the howls or the hum of the night creatures. The whole world became a scream.

She felt a hand land on her shoulder.

"Lily!"

She opened her eyes. There was her mother in her pajamas, looking concerned, backlit by the hall light.

"Honey, are you okay? You were screaming again."

Lily sat up. Her mouth tasted like she'd been drinking from the swamp, and her hands and feet were prickly and numb. The dream had felt so real. She'd been so sure that Britney was about to reach out and touch her, but here she was in bed under her covers, where everything was totally normal. For now. She cleared her throat.

"Nightmares," she croaked. Her voice was scratchy from the screaming.

Mom reached out to caress her head. "Do we need to take you to a doctor?"

Lily snorted. "Who do you see for this? It's just night-mares." *And if I told you what my nightmares were about, you would call me melodramatic and then have me committed,* she thought. *Not that we have the money for that anyway.*

"There are medications . . ."

But Lily shook her head. It wouldn't help. What if they made her stay asleep next time instead of screaming herself awake?

"No."

"Do you want me to stay with you tonight?"

Lily was breathing a sigh of relief and about to tell her yes when her father shouted from downstairs, "What's the little drama queen's problem now?"

Lily's mom sighed, and Lily hung her head. He hadn't shouted like that in a while, and it made her scared in a differ-ent way. When she was little and had nightmares, he'd been so kind and patient. But ever since Colorado, he hadn't had any comfort to offer her. Lily felt a wash of guilt, her shoulders hunching up. He just saw her as the thing that annoyed him at night, not as someone who needed help. At least Brian had liked Britney and had wanted to help her.

"I'll be okay," Lily lied.

"Are you sure?"

"Sure."

Because what other answer was there? It's not like the ghosts were limited to her room, and it's not like her mom could drive them away forever. Rachel's presence hadn't stopped Britney, after all. Lily shivered and snuggled more firmly under her covers to show her mom that she would be okay. She'd rather face ghosts than her dad being as angry as he was back in Colorado, the night she'd taken the drama too far.

Once her mom was back downstairs, Lily turned on her light and picked up a book. She stayed up all night, and as soon as the sun rose, she finally gave in to her fatigue. The moment her head hit the pillow, she fell asleep. This time, she didn't dream. Or if she did, she forgot all about it.

When she woke up in the afternoon, her knees were black with dust and her feet were sandy and covered in tiny cuts. This time, she wasn't surprised. With a strange sort of calm, she swept the gravel out of her sheets and dumped it in the bathroom trash can.

Lily knew only one thing for certain: She had to figure out how to give Britney what she wanted, or Britney was going to get rid of her permanently.

26.

WHEN LILY EMERGED FROM THE SHOWER AFTER WASHING ALL THE nightmare grime down the drain, she found her mom in the kitchen. Oddly, Mom seemed peppy and refreshed. Almost perky. It was like she'd completely forgotten the screaming incident last night.

"Good news!" Mom nearly sang. "Tomorrow's the big day. They found the storage container, and it arrives in the morning! And the dumpster leaves the next day. It's perfect." She put her hands on her hips and looked around the kitchen brightly. "This place will finally start to feel like a home. Like it's ours."

Lily shivered a little. Could it ever be *ours* when Britney thought of it as *mine*?

No matter how terrible it was, Lily had to accept that she was stuck here. Short of some kind of natural disaster, this was her life now. She just felt so helpless. Awake, asleep—she never felt safe. She couldn't even invite a friend over without them ending up in the hospital. And then unfriending her.

She didn't want to just wait around anymore. She had to figure out how to make peace with Britney. She had to give Britney what she wanted, which meant that she needed to know more—about Britney's life, and about her death.

Lily ate her cereal, only half listening to her mom prattling on about how great everything was. When she was done eating, she put on sneakers and went outside. Maybe seeing this place through Britney's eyes would help. First she went to the old pool, staring down into the green-black depths. Her dreams had brought her here, first in beautiful visions and then nearly killing her with grim reality. This place was important to Britney, a place where she'd been happy. But now it was abandoned and forgotten. If Britney wanted it, she could have it. There was nothing left of any value.

Next Lily brought some ham from the kitchen and went out toward the forest, calling for Buddy. Without his collar, she couldn't hear a jingle, and no matter how many times she whistled, he didn't show up. Shame stung her heart; she hadn't meant to kick him, but even he didn't believe her. Britney had mentioned Buddy multiple times. He'd meant a lot to her, and Britney was jealous that Lily kept playing with the dog she saw as still hers. If Buddy had shown up, Lily would've followed him into the woods to see where he'd been hiding and if maybe there were any clues to Britney's past there, but without him, she would just be wandering aimlessly in a dangerous place. Buddy had once comforted Britney, but now he comforted Lily, too.

As much as she didn't want to, she went to the dock next. She couldn't help picturing the scene Brian had described, the tragedy that had brought yellow caution tape to the pulpy gray boards and cemented Brian's own future. There wasn't much to see, just the same old boat and oars and the deceptively calm surface.

"What happened, Britney?" she said out loud. "Why did you drown?"

Lily half expected to feel cold hands shoving her into the water, but nothing touched her. There were no answers here. As soon as she backed onto the grass, she felt just a little bit safer, more solid. Looking toward the house, she wished Buddy hadn't taken the keys. Maybe there was something that would help her hidden behind the locked door under the stairs. But even though she searched all around the area where Buddy usually appeared, she didn't find them.

As Lily headed up to her room, she tried to think back to everything she'd tossed out when she'd cleaned the spare room, trying to recall if there might be any clues to why Britney had died. But most of it just seemed like relics from Brian's life before Britney. She hadn't seen any photos of Britney at all—

Wait.

Except she had, that first night, hadn't she? In the toilet. Photos of a little girl and a woman—probably her mother—their faces burned or scratched away. But those photos were in the bottom of the dumpster now, and surely the rain had utterly destroyed them.

In her room, she sat on her bed and looked around. It still felt like Britney's room, right down to the canvases on the walls. She took them off their nails and looked behind them, seeing if maybe Britney had hidden something there—more strange words, a key. Nothing. But Britney had written *MINE* on the bed. Did she want the bed back? She'd tossed it apart twice at least. She could have it, if that was what she wanted. As soon as the storage container arrived, Lily would be sleeping in her own bed again.

But it couldn't just be the bed. Britney hadn't mentioned it. Whatever she wanted had to be more personal.

Lily pulled down every book left on the shelf, checked the inside covers, and flipped through the pages. There was nothing of use, just Britney's name scrawled in the books that had been read the most. None of the books were underlined or highlighted or held any mementos. Several of the books were gone, and Lily had no idea why. She thought back to what the

MINE

room had looked like when she'd first arrived. The dead snake was in the dumpster. The drawers of clothes and the junk from the closet didn't seem important.

And then, all of a sudden, Lily knew what it was that Britney wanted so badly, what she needed to find peace.

Lily only hoped it wasn't too late.

27.

OF COURSE, IT WASN'T GOING TO BE EASY.

The storage container was arriving tomorrow, and Lily's mom needed her help getting everything ready. There was still trash that needed to go out, plus the grungy patio furniture and all the old clothes hanging in a few closets downstairs. With every load Lily threw away, her heart sank a little more. The thing she needed—her only hope for solving all her problems—was in the bottom of the dumpster. But every time she tried to climb the metal ladder up the dumpster's side, her mom called her away to do more chores. And there was no way she could explain to her mom that her goal was to get in the dumpster . . . and throw everything out again.

It was evening by the time her mom was satisfied that they were ready to bid the dumpster farewell. Lily was exhausted, filthy, and nervous. Sure, the days were long now, but the last thing she wanted was to be in that dumpster in the dark, alone at night.

"Why don't you guys go out to celebrate?" she said as her mom got dressed to pick up Dad at work. "You haven't been out in forever."

Her mom cocked her head and smiled like such a thing had never occurred to her. "But don't you want to celebrate, too? You've earned it. You've worked so hard to help me, and I know it hasn't been an easy move. And I can tell that you've tried to reduce the drama. I've noticed a real change in you, honey."

Lily forced herself to smile. It wasn't a change she'd meant to make at all. She hadn't really grown more normal and well-behaved; she was just anxious and scared. "Maybe bring me home some fast food? I'm too tired to act fancy. But you guys could go somewhere nice. You look like you need a steak."

Her mom started texting her dad, and when she put on her lipstick and mascara, Lily exhaled a sigh of relief. The moment the car was out of sight, she put on jeans and sneakers and grabbed her dad's small but powerful flashlight. She went out into the driveway and stared at the big metal box that she'd spent so much time filling up. She didn't have long, but now she had to get past all that junk, down to the very bottom. And it wasn't going to be fun. At least her fingertips had healed.

The metal rungs on the dumpster were rough and hurt her hands, but she climbed up and stared down at all the garbage inside, trying to plan the best approach. She remembered tossing the first few black bags onto the far side, which at least meant she might not have to move hundreds of pounds of cardboard boxes out of the way. She slung a leg over the metal edge and took a deep breath. There was no ladder on the inside. Whether or not she found what she was looking for, climbing back out was not going to be easy.

She shook her head and climbed back down to the gravel. There was an old wooden ladder in the garage, so she fetched it and dragged it over. It took all her strength to lift it up over the dumpster's edge and let it topple onto the stack of boxes, but at least now she had a chance of getting out again. Her parents were going to be mad no matter what, but it would be better if they didn't find her stuck and screaming for help inside a half-emptied dumpster.

This time, as Lily perched on the edge of the big metal box, six feet off the ground, the sun was just beginning to set. She was terrified but determined. If she was right, maybe Britney would leave her alone for good and she could try to have a normal life here. If she was wrong . . . well, the best-case scenario was getting found in a dumpster, covered in garbage, by parents who already thought she was the world's biggest drama queen. The worst-case scenario was either being killed by a ghost or being crushed by garbage and becoming a ghost herself. Lily tried not to think too hard about the worst-case scenarios. She had to do this, so she would do it.

She had never considered herself a particularly brave person, but she knew well enough by now how to act brave. The very first time she'd gone onstage, she'd been so scared she'd almost chickened out, but she'd since learned to love that thrill of excitement in her belly, the way her eyes felt too bright and her feet felt cold right before she stepped into the heat of the lights.

Looking down into the depths of the dumpster, she reminded herself of Miss Cora's words. This was just like stage fright. The only way to deal with real fright was to feel the fear and do it anyway.

There were no bright stage lights here, only the bare bulb on the side of the house that wouldn't turn on anymore, but still Lily stepped down onto the stack of folded cardboard boxes like she had an audience watching her every move. She was tough and strong. She was Angelica and she was Puck and she was Ariel and she was Veronica and she was Cady and she was Lydia and she was as agile as any cat in *Cats*.

Or not.

The moment her foot hit the top cardboard box, she slipped and fell. It was mushy and slick with rain, and she scrambled to slide to the far side so that she'd at least be near her goal. It was awful, tumbling and landing in a damp pile of black garbage bags. She couldn't tell what was in each one, but she could feel sharp bits and hard bits and mushy bits, and the smell made her want to throw up. They'd been throwing their own garbage in here, too.

She found her footing, grabbed the nearest bag, and heaved it up and over the side of the dumpster. Then another. Then another. They were heavy and wet and covered in leaves and grime, and it was apparently a lot easier putting things in than taking things out. Each time a bag landed on the ground outside, Lily couldn't help wincing; she was going to have to toss them back in or face her angry parents. But she couldn't let that stop her. Even as her arms burned and her legs ached, she kept on tossing things out of the dumpster, aiming to reach the floor of the far corner. She sang "Yo Girl" from *Heathers,* imagining an audience of ghosts cheering her on, helping her avoid the true danger. It didn't really work, but it felt good to sing.

With each bag or box, she felt less fear and a little bit more hope. It was just work, she told herself—not impossible. It was difficult and gross, but it wasn't as bad as the black water of the pool or the thick boggy ground of the swamp, and she'd gotten through those, hadn't she? At one point, she stopped to stare at a trio of sandhill cranes flying into the brilliant sunset overhead, and it crossed her mind that if she wasn't being haunted, she might actually enjoy living here. But as the last bit of light faded away, she realized that she had to hurry even more. Her parents could be home at any time, and they would want answers.

Of course, Britney could show up anytime, too.

Lily pulled the flashlight out of her pocket and flicked it

on. It wasn't fun, holding it in her mouth as she dug through the garbage bags, but it was better than being alone in complete darkness, which is what would happen soon. It was almost like the sun could sense her unease, as the sunset seemed to hold on for a long moment, the sky a gentle purple-gray that ever so slowly faded away to indigo.

And then full night fell like a velvet curtain.

The moon would be a tiny sliver when it rose. The stars sparked bright, popping out one at a time, and Lily paused to watch them. Since moving here, she hadn't bothered to spend much time looking at the night sky, but it was different than it had been back home in Boulder. Colorado's stars seemed close, the sky so wide and endless. Here, the trees crowded around like a picture frame, and the stars twinkled proudly, high up and distant. If she could solve this problem, free herself from this strange, ghostly cage, maybe she would have a chance to enjoy the night again instead of dreading it.

She went back to tossing bags, now with a renewed sense of panic. Dark was Britney's time. Dark was when the shadows seemed to move and shift like water and oil mixing, when she couldn't trust what was real and what wasn't. But this was real, she told herself. She had chosen to do this. And if she screamed, no warm hand would wake her. She was completely alone.

Some of the bags were too heavy to toss, so she shoved them

away, toward the boxes near the ladder. She found familiar pieces of furniture, an old vacuum, a broken chair. Her arms burned from lifting so much, and her legs were drenched with collected rain from the plastic bags and who even knew what else. She was getting closer and closer to her goal. She found the old aquarium, almost cut herself on the broken glass. At least the dead snake was still inside it, not rattling around in the dumpster with her.

She stopped for a moment to wipe the sweat out of her eyes.

And then she heard the sound she'd been dreading.

Just a voice, but it made her blood run cold.

"I told you to go away."

28.

LILY COULDN'T TELL WHERE THE VOICE WAS COMING FROM, SO SHE just picked up her pace. Desperately now, she ripped bags up from the pile, strained under their weight, and threw them out of the dumpster with a grunt. She pulled the flashlight out of her mouth and shoved it in her armpit, clenching her arm. If she lost it, she wouldn't have any way to see.

"I can't go away," she said, trying to keep her voice calm, reasonable, and bright like Glinda the Good Witch. "I'm a kid. My parents live here, so I have to live here, too."

Yank, toss, thump, shove, yank, toss.

Her arms and shoulders ached from the heavy bags, but she couldn't stop.

She almost dropped the flashlight and resettled it.

"I don't like this," Britney warned. "I don't like what you're doing. You should go to sleep so we can play."

Lily shook her head but didn't stop her work.

She hadn't let herself think too deeply about it, but now understanding rushed in.

All these dreams she'd been having, even the nice ones—was that Britney's work, too? Was Britney . . . possessing her? Is that how she could swim and whistle so naturally? Could Britney be . . .

. . . inside her?

She shuddered at the thought and went back to work. She was getting so close now. She yanked Britney's old comforter out of the stack—it was soaking wet and heavy, going dark with mildew and rot—and hefted it over the edge of the dumpster. It splatted in the sandy dirt below.

"Playing is fun," Lily said, trying to buy time. "Maybe we could be friends."

She heard the creaking thumps of someone climbing up the ladder outside, the sound of water dripping down the rusted metal.

"I don't have friends," Britney said, her voice sharp with scorn. And hurt. "They don't like me. Only Buddy likes me."

Lily started pawing the black bags apart, hunting for the right one. It had to be near here. It would be soft, nothing hard or heavy at all. Just a child's collection of clothes. And stuffed animals.

"I know," she told Britney. "Buddy is a good dog."

Britney sighed, and her breath sounded thick and wet, like she had pneumonia. "He didn't mean to do it," she said softly.

"Do what?"

Britney went still behind her, but Lily didn't stop in her own work, just kept tearing at the bags, hunting for the right one as she listened.

"I was fishing on the dock and I fell over. I didn't mean to. Mama said to not ever tell anybody about the fall-overs. That they would take me away and give me bad medicine. So I didn't tell Grampa Brian. I hid it from him. I didn't know I was gonna do a fall-over. But I did, and I fell in the water, and Buddy jumped in and tried to help me. But he just kept hitting me with his paws, and I couldn't stop doing the fall-over. I never can. It feels bad. It hurts my teeth."

Lily thought she knew what Britney was talking about.

"Epilepsy?" she asked, goose bumps crawling over her skin. "Is that what you had? Seizures?"

"Yeah," Britney said really softly. "The fall-overs."

Lily didn't stop shoving bags and garbage aside, but she felt tears well up in her eyes. This poor little kid, keeping a secret like that. And because of it, she died. For no reason. No wonder she was so angry.

"That stinks," Lily said, totally honest and not acting at all. "But I'm going to find Mine for you. That's what I'm doing right now. That's what you need, right? He's in here, somewhere."

"She!" Britney shouted, all softness gone. "She!"

There was a soft, wet thump behind her.

Britney—whatever Britney was now—*was in the dumpster with her.*

29.

LILY TOOK A DEEP BREATH AND SCRAMBLED FOR THE NEXT BAG. BUT when she went to toss it out of the dumpster, it didn't quite make it. The bag bounced back inside, knocking her over.

The cardboard boxes on the other side shifted as Britney slid deeper among the bags.

Lily shook her head and refocused. She had to do this. She reached down and felt around and ripped open a black plastic bag. She was so sure it was the right one, but it just held old curtains, thick and graying white. She tried to toss the open bag aside and nearly lost her flashlight. The curtains unfurled around her, tangling her up, and she thrashed and cried out as the memories descended.

The last time she'd seen curtains like this had been in Colorado, at Mr. Smith's house. Mr. Smith was Dad's boss, had been for ten years, and he'd invited them over for the annual

Christmas party. It was the first year Lily was old enough to attend, and she had gone into a monologue for the adults, showing off her mastery of Shakespeare, swirling the hem of the long curtain around her like Titania's dress, and then the curtain touched a nearby candle, and . . .

No. She couldn't go there. She had to focus on Britney now.

"She," Lily choked out as she untangled herself from the curtains and pushed them away. It was just too much, adding the guilt and shame of the past to her current fears all at once. Britney seemed to slow down whenever Lily was talking, so she just kept going. "I'm sorry. Yeah. Because Mine is your pink bunny. She. I'm looking for her right now. I bet you really miss her."

"You threw her away. You took Buddy's collar, too," Britney accused. "You want to take my stuff."

"I didn't know," Lily argued. "I'm trying to find the collar, too. I don't know where my mom put it. I'm trying to make it right." She glanced at the curtains again, remembering the numbness she'd felt, standing outside Mr. Smith's house under a firefighter blanket as the artisan-polished wood walls went up in flames, destroying everything in front of her dad's entire office crowd. "I'm trying to make everything right, but it's so hard."

On the far side of the dumpster, the cardboard boxes shifted again. One slammed into Lily's back.

She had to stall Britney before she made it across the dumpster.

"My mom took my stuff." Britney sounded so sullen, so angry. Lily could feel pressure building in the sky again, and everything went a shade darker, the clouds covering the scant light of the moon and stars.

"Did she?" Lily prompted.

"Mama took things," Britney growled. "That's why I scratched her out of the pictures and threw them in the potty. I didn't want to see her anymore. She was mean. But she never took Mine. *You* did that."

"I know," Lily agreed softly. "And I'm sorry. I'm going to fix it. Promise."

Behind her, where she didn't dare look, she could hear the soft, heavy weight of a body working its way across the leftovers of two broken lives, wading through bags of junk. No more time to toss out bags. She felt around for a soft one and ripped it open. No—just old towels and artificial flowers.

"You can't fix it. It's too late. But we can play. I like it when we play. You see better than I did. I swim better than you can. It's fun to be you."

Bile rose in Lily's throat as she thought about her dreams, about floating in the blue water, about how she'd started reading books she'd never liked before and how she could suddenly whistle with two fingers and knew how to tie on a fishhook. Those things . . .

How did she know those things?

She remembered now. It all came back. It was like being in the audience, recalling what it felt like to angrily strip the bed or sit on the dock at night, throwing her own books far out into the water. She could still taste the paper from when she'd torn up and eaten the note she'd written to Britney. She could see it so clearly, see exactly what her hands had looked like as they reached out on their own to shove Rachel down the stairs.

Thump.

Something hit the trash bags right behind her.

So, so close behind her.

Lily reached for the next black bag, the one on the very bottom of the dumpster. She ripped it open, and shirts tumbled out.

Small shirts, still folded.

It was the right bag.

She fell to her knees on the bottom of the dumpster and plunged her hands into the bag. But she was so frantic that she forgot the flashlight under her armpit. It clattered into the shadows below the trash and clanked against the metal, rolling out of sight. The bags behind her hit her back, and a piece of cardboard slid overhead like the lid of a coffin. A cold, wet hand landed on her arm, squeezing hard.

"Mama said I was bad, but I'm not bad. And I don't want to be alone anymore," Britney whispered.

Lily yanked her arm away and felt around in the plastic

bag, racking her memory for each of the stuffed animals she'd tossed. Not this doll, not that horse, not this hippo.

There! She couldn't see anything, but she could feel it. A dirty pink bunny with floppy, torn ears. And across its belly in faded, ripped embroidery, the words she hadn't quite noticed: *Be Mine*. She grabbed it and spun around, holding it in front of her like a shield as she knocked the cardboard box aside to reveal the sky.

"Here she is, Britney," she said. "Mine. I'm sorry I took her from you."

In that tiny amount of light, Lily could see a body standing just above her in the dumpster. A girl, small for eight years old, her hair cut jagged by an old man's trembling hands. Her skin looked too puffy, and water dripped steadily from her wet clothes. Her face was hidden in shadow, and Lily had never been more grateful for anything in her entire life.

"Mine," Britney whispered, and it was gentle and soft.

Cold fingers scraped against Lily's hands, taking the bunny away.

And then, in between one breath and the next, Britney was gone.

30.

THE ENTIRE WORLD CHANGED IN THAT INSTANT. THE CLOUDS LIFTED. The moon and stars shone down. The night's soft noises rose on hot, honeysuckle-heavy air. And the outside bulb that had refused to work clicked on, flooding the dumpster with golden light.

Lily looked around, making sure Britney was gone. There was no visible sign that she'd even been here, other than some wet spots on the pile of cardboard boxes. But everything just . . . felt different.

Before, it felt like someone had always stood behind Lily, watching her. Like she could get lost at any moment, like the very land repelled her. Now it just felt like . . . a normal place. No malevolence, no strange pressure, no evil. She took a deep breath, filling her lungs with air, and it was like she hadn't been able to breathe for days.

Like she'd been invisible.

Like she'd been drowning.

Like maybe she hadn't been able to breathe properly since she started the blaze that burned down her dad's boss's house and got her dad fired, his reputation destroyed. It didn't matter how many counselors had told her it wasn't her fault—her dad had decided it was, and so it was.

That thought had clamped down on her, dominating everything, at least until Britney arrived.

But if she could make Britney go away, maybe she could banish the ghost of what she'd done, too.

She reached down and picked up the fallen flashlight, tucking it in her pocket so her dad wouldn't yell. And that was another revelation—knowing that the worst thing that might happen that night was getting yelled at by her dad over a flashlight.

Lily hurried back toward the other end of the dumpster, stood the wooden ladder up, even though it wobbled, and clambered up toward the sturdier metal ladder outside. She toppled the wooden ladder over the edge and back onto the ground, climbed down, and went to work tossing the black bags and old lamps and garbage back inside the dumpster. It wasn't easy, and half the bags had broken open like rotten pumpkins, but she scrambled to clean up as much as possible before her parents got home from their date.

Much to her surprise, she succeeded. Thank goodness it was a long date. She even had time to put the ladder back in the detached garage. By the time the car rolled into the driveway, there was almost no sign of what had happened in the dumpster, as long as nobody looked inside it. When they came in the house, her parents found Lily sitting on the couch inside, reading a book as if nothing at all had happened.

Well, mostly.

"What on earth is that smell?" her mom asked as she put her purse on the counter.

Lily looked down. Uh-oh. She had forgotten about that part. She was still covered in dumpster juice.

"I did some more cleaning," she said. "Just trying to make sure everything is ready for tomorrow."

Her dad shook his head at her. "Well, go take a shower. You smell like garbage, drama queen."

Lily smiled. She couldn't even be annoyed with him right now. To the outside observer, smelling like rotten garbage actually *was* a bit dramatic.

"Yes, sir," she said, saluting him before marching off for a shower and fresh pajamas.

The bathroom felt safe and clean, but when she saw the small green-black handprint on the back of her arm, reality came crashing down.

It had happened. It was really real.

And it was over.

She stood under the hot water, scrubbing and scrubbing until her skin was red.

For the first time in months, she allowed in the dark thoughts, the memories of what had happened in Colorado, that night at the Smiths' house. She remembered how much she was loving the spotlight, having so many adults enraptured by her monologue and impressed with her memory and skills, commenting that surely she was too young for Shakespeare, and then she remembered that first hiss as the curtains caught fire and the flames leapt straight up to lick the wood ceiling.

She could still feel her dad's hands on her arms, yanking her away as the fire tried to jump to her dress, and all the adults moving in to beat the fire away or try to stop it with a tiny extinguisher from the kitchen. But the fire grew so fast. The house had been built like a fancy log cabin, all gleaming honey-tan wood and natural fabrics. Everyone had to run outside in a burst of black smoke, a hundred people screaming and crying and hysterical, the entire party huddling by their parked cars, too horrified to move. She remembered every word Mr. Smith shouted into his phone, demanding that the fire department hurry and then screaming so hard at Dad about his stupid, terrible, foolish, idiotic daughter that Dad ended up crying right there in public, something Lily didn't even think was possible.

"You're a bad kid," Mr. Smith had said to her right before they drove off, the fire flashing off teeth bared like an animal's.

And her dad? He hadn't argued.

Since then, they'd had lots of talks. About responsibility. About less drama. About being normal. About being good. But what Lily had heard, over and over again, was that she was bad. That the fire and everything else that had happened—her dad losing his job and being unable to get another, thanks to Mr. Smith's rage; their family having to move down here to escape the embarrassment around town—were her fault. She'd come to believe that there was something wrong with who she was.

But now Lily saw it clearly. She was just a kid, and kids made mistakes.

Terrible ones sometimes.

But mistakes were mistakes, and accidents were accidents. It was true for Britney, and it was true for Lily.

The next morning, a big truck backed down the driveway and brought the storage container that held all of their belongings. A fleet of college guys in matching T-shirts carried everything inside, and when Lily's mom offered them some extra cash, they carried out all the old furniture that had come with the house. Britney's bed, the old sofa, the ancient recliner. They tossed it all in the dumpster until it was overflowing. And then the next day, another big truck backed down the driveway and took the dumpster away, leaving nothing behind but a rectangle of dead brown grass.

The house was completely different once they had their

own furniture and towels and artwork in place. Working together, all three of them, they got the TV hooked up to the Wi-Fi and set up the desktop and put down rugs to cover the dusty wooden floorboards. They hung paintings and unpacked boxes. Lily had never really thought much about decorating or her mom's obsession with throw pillows, but now she recognized the wonderful feeling of familiarity, of home. Of how a thing went from *someone else's* to *mine*.

Her dad was in a great mood—better than Lily had seen in months. When she tentatively asked if they could order pizza for dinner, he agreed and even ordered the big meal with breadsticks and dessert and soda. They ate at the kitchen table using their own dishes and silverware, and when they were done, Lily offered to take her dad's plate.

"I see you trying," he told her, meeting her eyes. "I know it's been hard. But I've seen you cleaning, and I saw you working today. You're doing a good job. I know you miss Colorado . . ." He trailed off and had to look away for a moment, but then he refocused on her, his face softening. "But I think we're going to be okay here."

He saw her again.

He finally saw her.

And when he saw her, he found something to like.

Lily felt the relief like a ball of sunshine in her chest and dared to do a little stage bow. He played along with a golf clap.

Maybe they would never get back to where they'd been when she was little, and maybe he would never apologize for how he'd made her feel all this time . . . but maybe they could find some way to meet in the middle.

That night, she slept in her own bed, surrounded by her books and posters and stuffed animals. Her dreams were just normal dreams, and she felt no fear at all as she drifted off.

She knew that Britney was gone.

"This house is mine now," she whispered to the darkness. And then, in the tiniest whisper, "And I'm not bad, either."

31.

A FEW DAYS LATER, RACHEL PARKED HER BOAT AT THE DOCK AND hopped out as if nothing strange had ever happened, aside from the hot-pink cast on her right arm. Lily had texted most of the story to Rachel, and Rachel had finally agreed to come over again, if only to hear every melodramatic detail in person. Lily wasn't sure if Rachel believed her or had just appreciated the overall drama of the tale, but it turned out that Rachel was curious and had done a bit of internet research while she was recovering from her fall. What Lily told her fit well enough with what she'd learned, and she wanted to explore the property some more.

"The ghosts are gone," Lily said, smiling. "Promise."

Not that she was ever going to trust the dock.

Since that night in the dumpster, she hadn't had a bad dream, seen anything creepy, heard voices, or encountered anything even remotely paranormal. Yeah, she'd seen a few more giant roaches, but they were definitely from the natural world and not part of some ghostly conspiracy. They were still gross, though.

"It really does look different. So cute," Rachel said, looking around as Lily glowed with pride over how pretty the house looked. "But I want to hear everything. Everything!"

So Lily took her to the little door on the side of the house. Her father had used some trick he found online to pick the lock, and when he opened the door, he hadn't really understood what was inside. But Lily had.

It was Britney's secret place, lit by a single lightbulb, and the yellow-painted walls were covered in marker drawings. In some of the drawings, a stick figure that had to be Britney's mom was frowning, and in some, she had devil horns. Here was Britney with her mom, living in a car. There was Britney at school, with other little kids pointing and laughing at her. There she lay on the floor, frowning, eyes closed, with little lines all around her to show she was shaking with a seizure. Here she was swimming and playing with Buddy and watching TV with Grampa Brian in the recliners, all smiling and happy. And in every single childish drawing, again and again, there was that same stuffed pink bunny with the floppy ears and the words *Be Mine* stitched on his tummy.

"He made this place for her," Lily said. "The house was his, but he created this special little place for her so she could have something all her own. She was used to living in a car. So it probably felt more like home."

"This is so wild," Rachel said softly, running a hand over the drawings. "The poor kid. I mean, I don't forgive her for pushing me down the stairs and breaking three bones, but still. It's just so sad."

"At least she was happy for a while," Lily said. "They both were. It was just an accident."

They crawled out and stood, and Lily closed the door. This was one part of the house that didn't need to change. Her mom had wanted to paint over the drawings and use it for storage, but Lily had managed to talk her out of it. She was Britney's last audience, her *only* audience, and she of all people understood what a responsibility that was. Maybe only Lily would ever truly know and understand Britney's story, and she wanted to show it the respect it deserved.

But since Britney had caused Rachel harm, she thought Rachel deserved to know, too, and so she was glad to share the burden. She took Rachel up to her newly decorated room and stopped to show her that her father had glued the trick step down, claiming that it wobbled too much to be safe.

"You're right," Rachel finally said. "It does feel totally different. Like a different house. But whatever happened to the dog? Did he run away for good?"

Lily pointed to the forest. "I haven't seen him in a couple

of days. Maybe he ran away or got picked up by animal control or something."

Rachel cocked her head, her old curious grin coming back. "Let's go see!"

Lily didn't really want to go into the forest, but she wanted to be friends with Rachel again, so she would've agreed to just about anything. When Rachel loped toward the woods, Lily followed along.

It was hard going, overgrown with thick grasses and prickly undergrowth and sharp trees, but Rachel was determined. Lily followed her deeper into the forest, and when Rachel found a little path, barely more than a deer trail, they headed down it. Lily was paranoid, looking everywhere for another snake or an alligator—she'd seen a few small ones, around the lake. But Rachel was undeterred.

"Buddy!" she called. "Here, boy!"

Lily called, too, and even tried that old two-fingered whistle, although she couldn't quite do it anymore.

Within a few minutes, she heard a low whine. Lily sped up, tearing through the undergrowth. She pushed past Rachel and burst into a clearing.

She couldn't believe what she saw.

There was Buddy, just sitting there, clean and sleek. He was wearing his collar. At his feet sat the ring of keys with the rabbit's foot.

"Buddy?" Lily said, and as if some spell had broken, he

leapt up and trotted to her, licking her hand happily before standing on his back legs and putting his paws on her shoulders.

"Wow, he *is* friendly!" Rachel said. "I thought he was scared of everything!"

Buddy politely hopped down and went to give Rachel a lick, and Lily noticed something on the ground where he'd been sitting, half buried in a messy dirt hole, like Buddy was trying to dig it out.

The hairs rose along her arms as she knelt and pulled it free. It was a small wooden box, simple but beautifully made. Carved into the top was the name *Britney West*. Lily traced a finger over the words, imagining Brian's old, spotted hands holding a carving knife as he cried.

"What's that?" Rachel asked.

Lily didn't say anything. She just opened the box to show a tightly sealed bag containing powdery gray ashes.

Britney's remains.

"Buddy's been protecting her, all this time," she said softly.

When she stood back up, she realized she was crying. Rachel put a hand on her back and then hugged her. As they stood there, sobbing in the forest under the hot August sun, Buddy sat quietly, leaning into their legs, his tail wagging gently.

Sometime later, Rachel asked her, "What next?"

Lily looked around, feeling like she was finally in control of her life again.

"The show must go on," she said with a shrug.

Cradling the wooden box, Lily walked back toward the house with Rachel and Buddy by her side. The girls put the ashes in Britney's little cabinet under the stairs, and Lily used the key ring to lock the door again. All the while, Buddy stayed nearby, watching and wagging his tail.

"What are you going to do about him?" Rachel asked.

Lily smiled, petting his shaggy brown head.

"Take care of him," she said. "With Britney gone, he needs someone. I think she would've wanted it that way, in the end. No more being invisible, hiding under all that mud, having people say he's a bad dog. No more being alone."

After only a minor flounce and major tantrum, her parents agreed to let him stay.

There were benefits to being a drama queen, after all.

ACKNOWLEDGMENTS

This book was written mostly on my back on a heating pad while typing with a pinched nerve because I thought it was perfectly reasonable to open my car trunk before leaving for Disney World. I have never regretted opening a car trunk more. I was in a lot of pain and couldn't feel the fingers on my left hand. Thank you, car, for giving me a unique perspective when writing my first horror novel for kids.

Thanks to my husband, Craig, for always supporting my writing and putting up with me shouting at the dictation software when I couldn't type anymore. Thanks to my mom, Linda, for not noticing when I borrowed her horror books as a kid after she told me they were too scary for me. Thanks to my own kids, Rex and Rhys, for just being flat-out wonderful and for agreeing with me that the house our very nice neighbors live in would make a great haunted house. Thanks to our very nice neighbors, April and Carol, for letting us fish on your dock, which is not actually haunted.

Probably.

Thanks to my agent, Stacia Decker, for helping me dial up the creepy on this book before finding it a great home. Thanks to my editor, Wendy Loggia, for believing in it and finding a way to make it even creepier. Thanks to Alison Romig and everyone on the Delacorte Press team for an incredible experience. Thanks to Corey Brickley for creating the perfect cover that makes me even more terrified of mirrors. And thanks to my copy editor, Kathleen Reed, for letting me use *possum* instead of *opossum,* which no one in Florida says, and also for pointing out that I'd used the word *crusted* fifty times. Yes, there is a lot of crust in the book, but I appreciate the chance to find more adjectives. All y'all helped make this book better, and I wish I could buy you a box of doughnuts to share with a really good dog.

Thanks to Katherine Arden, Chuck Wendig, and Greg van Eekhout for advice around writing middle grade, and thanks to Kevin Hearne for constant writing encouragement and that amazing drawing of a capybara.

When I was a kid, my favorite scary book was *Ghost Cat.* I hope this book haunts you like *Ghost Cat* still haunts me.

<3,

d

ABOUT THE AUTHOR

Delilah S. Dawson thought she would be a visual artist but somehow ended up a writer. She grew up in Roswell, Georgia, and has lived all around the South, including Tampa, near where this book takes place. She has worked as a muralist, an art teacher, a barista, a reptile caretaker, a project manager, and a dead body in a haunted house, which was probably the most fun. She is the *New York Times* bestselling author of *Star Wars: Phasma* and fourteen other books for teens and adults, as well as the comics *Ladycastle, Sparrowhawk,* and *Star Pig.* She loves gluten-free cake, having adventures, the beach, Disney World, and vintage My Little Pony. She once kissed a camel named Louis.

whimsydark.com